My friend Mary

will

always be w

you In His love,

gail

May 2012

# The Time for Grace

Gail Iverson

*CrossBooks™*
*A Division of LifeWay*
*1663 Liberty Drive*
*Bloomington, IN 47403*
*www.crossbooks.com*
*Phone: 1-866-879-0502*



*First published by CrossBooks 2/6/2012*

*ISBN: 978-1-4627-1302-8 (sc)*
*ISBN: 978-1-4627-1304-2 (hc)*
*ISBN: 978-1-4627-1303-5 (e)*

*Library of Congress Control Number: 2011963559*

*Printed in the United States of America*

*This is dedicated with love to*
*Abigail, Peyton, Carsen, Sedona, and Alexis.*
*May you always cling to the One who gives grace*
*and love unconditionally.*

*May my life song be a song of love to You.*

*Every life is a song, through our unique DNA, we weave a melody. My song started out as an innocent harmony in my youth. As I reached adolescence it found the minor keys of life. By God's grace, my life found the rhapsody of His love—forever praise His Name!*

# Chapter 1

Journey with me, will you, to my childhood? You know, those summer days that in our minds seemed to go on forever? How I remember waking to the smell of lilacs outside my bedroom window on a sun drenched summer morning, bacon frying downstairs, and the sharp aroma of my dad's coffee perking in the silver coffee maker that sat bubbling over our GE electric stove. Oh yes, and my mother's singing, wafting through the house, with a comfort that made everything in this little girls life just right.

I was the youngest of three siblings, and probably the "whoops" child, although that never stopped me from feeling fully loved, and a bit spoiled from two adoring siblings. A Midwest child, from a good old down to earth, salt of the earth, home grown, strong work ethic, stay at home mom, kind of a family. My father loomed large in our house. He demanded respect, and got it. The smell of Old Spice aftershave still brings me back to simpler times, innocent days, when I wanted nothing more in a day than to make my dad proud of me; to hear his laugh, his approval.

Can you recall those days of running through sprinklers, spitting watermelon seeds, and that delicious time between afternoon shadows and dusk falling, when you hear your mom calling you to supper, and you want to stay and wait for the fireflies to come out and play? Warm summer afternoons, shouting over the fence to a neighbor friend, "Can you play?" Lying on your backs, pointing up to cumulus cotton balls, finding an elephant, and watching it morph into a leaping jaguar.

How easy it is to slip back to those days of front porch swings, fresh mown grass, the laughter of young girls washing dishes in the kitchen . . .

My life changed when I was fourteen. Not an easy age for a young girl, as I began entering the world of womanhood, and not sure if I wanted to go. Life was changing whether I wanted it to or not. Both of my siblings had already left home, and I was trying to figure out what my friends found so fascinating in boys.

I wasn't a beauty, but more a gangly teenager who fought acne flare ups now and then. I did somehow get attention from the opposite gender. I had wanted long hair all my life, and was finally allowed to grow out my blonde hair until it swished down my back straight and thick, sometimes caught back in a pony tail. Dad wanted me to stay a little girl; mom gently reminded him that I was growing up.

Perhaps my mom named me Grace after one of her favorite movie stars, the classy and exquisite Grace Kelley. Or perhaps she knew in her mother's heart that I was a child that would need lots and lots of grace.

So, on a rainy November evening, when shade trees were skeletal and even the resilient evergreen swayed in the brisk autumn evening, my world was altered in a way never to return to innocence.

# Chapter 2

I was home alone, something that rarely happened. Listening to the rain battering the roof like a hail of bullets, I was wishing my family would get home. That morning, my parents and two sisters left for a Christmas shopping adventure in a nearby town. My mom had been looking forward to time with her girls, one who had recently married and moved away. Now I was scrambling through my memory trying to remember when exactly my dad said they would be home.

The jarring ringing of the phone pounded in my chest. Doesn't it sometimes seem that the ringing of a phone produces different tones, almost as if we can sense by the ring something is wrong?

I answered it in the proper way I was taught by my father. "Norman residence, may I help you?" Believing that my dad would be on the other end explaining why they were late.

"Is this Grace Norman?"

"Uh, yeah"

"Grace, I am a nurse at St. Mark's Hospital. Your father has asked me to call you, and instructed for you to go to your neighbor's house. You need to ask them to take you to the hospital right away."

"Oh, okay. Uh, which neighbor?"

"Do you know where the Kirkland's live? That is where your father would like you to go."

"Yeah. Okay."

"Grace, come to the emergency room, and let them know who you are."

"Okay. Bye. Thanks"

I felt my heart drumming a crazy beat in my chest as I tried clearing my mind. An upbeat commercial jingle came on the TV and for a brief moment gave me a sense of normality.

Looking down at what I was wearing, I tried thinking through what my mom would tell me to do. Change to a better outfit, turn off the TV; turn out the lights? Oh, maybe just some of them.

The Kirkland's lived next door, and even though I didn't know them well, they seemed like a nice older couple. The wind dampened with rain whipped my hair and I ran back in the house for a coat. I knocked on the Kirkland's door and waited for what seemed like forever, while the first cold clutch of unease worked its way up my spine.

Mrs. Kirkland flipped on the front porch light. Her uncertain look made me realize what I must look like, knocking on their door at night in the pouring rain, looking a bit uncertain myself. After explaining what I had been told, she hollered, "Les, I'm taking Grace to the hospital. Her family has been in an accident." *An accident . . . what could have happened*? All kinds of imagery fluttered through my mind. I think her saying the word accident made it all more real.

The ride to the hospital seemed all a blur, although I remember her talking in nervous nonsensical phrases. The droning of her voice was comforting, and kept my own thoughts from going down trails I didn't want to explore. The emergency room was a flurry of activity, nurses, doctors, and patients. Mrs. Kirkland held my hand as I was led into a small sterile room. A doctor's office, I presumed. A tall white coat walked in with a weary but kind face attached. Without much introduction, he called for some water and gave me a pill, and I took it without question. I sat across from him, a cluttered desk in between us.

"Grace, I'm Dr. Michelson. I was the doctor on call when your family was brought in. As you heard, your family has been in an accident. I'm not aware of the details, Grace, but you may want to get the details from the police report later. Your father has a concussion, several broken bones, and a few minor cuts and scrapes. Your sister, Katie, has a broken hip and a few minor breaks. Your other sister Shelley broke her pelvis, and is a little loopy right now from a hit to the head. They all are pretty banged up, but we fully expect them to recover."

Processing what I was hearing, I sighed with relief, running the 'we fully expect them to recover' in my mind. The doctor looked tired, worn. He started to speak, hesitated, and then glanced down at his hands. Surgeon hands. Strong, capable. There was an awkward silence.

Unsure of how to respond, I stammered, "Okay, thanks. Thanks for your help. Um, can I see them?"

"Grace. It's your mom. She was dead on arrival."

The room started to spin. I heard someone cry "NO!" and realized it came from my trembling mouth. From somewhere Mrs. Kirkland materialized and I felt her hand clasp mine. The room was claustrophobic, too small to contain all the overwhelming emotions in it. The doctor laid a comforting hand on my shoulder. Nodding to Mrs. Kirkland, he guided me through the halls to see my sister, Katie. Tubes, stitches and bruises didn't distract from the fact that Katie knew about mom. Silent tears streamed down her face. "Gracie, it's mama."

"I know. I know." At a loss for words, we both stared out from pained eyes to the white walls, and the knowledge that our lives would never be the same.

The ride home was dismal. My reflection in the car window illuminated every time we passed under a street lamp. The reflection looked hollow, fearful, and the tears were hard to discern from the rain drops creeping down the window.

Mrs. Kirkland patted my knee as we pulled into her driveway. "Honey, this has been a terrible night for you, but God will help you through this. Go to Him for your strength."

*God? So, this God is going to help me through after He snatched my mom from me? Right.*

And then there were all the arrangements. Picking out the funeral home, the burial plot, what my mother would wear, all the murky details. My father's sister, Aunt Emma, helped with arrangements, as if we were planning a party. Uncle Will spent his time testing the constant influx of neighbor's and friend's casseroles. I remember nodding when appropriate, and waiting for the nightmare to be over. It was all such a surreal emptiness. The burial plot was under a stately oak tree. Her dress was a light shade of green that she had been so proud of when she bought it for Shelley's graduation. The casket was mahogany, with brass handles and a soft velvet lining.

And there we were, on a cold November afternoon, the sky ominous as we shivered by the grave. The gray gunmetal sky matched the bleakness of my soul. Clenching Aunt Emma's hand, the words of the minister floated over my head. There was such a severe contrast between my outward being and the agony within. My hesitant smile responded to all of the, "Poor, sweet Grace. Are you going to be alright?"

Nodding, yes, "All is fine".

"Dear, sweet girl, such a great loss."

"I'll be fine. Uncle Will and Aunt Emma are taking great care of me. My family will be home from the hospital soon."

"If there is anything I can do . . ."

*Bring my mother back! No, mama! Don't leave me. I can't live without you. Please let me wake up from this nightmare. Please come back.*

"What a terrible tragedy. Just call if you need anything."

"No, I'm fine. Thanks so much for coming."

*Mama, it is so cold. Come back. Make me warm. Please don't leave me. Oh, help me! I can't do this.*

"Yes, I'm okay. Thank you for coming."

Getting through that first Thanksgiving, Christmas, and New Year's was unbelievably painful. Having a mother die in November, left our family with a triple gut punch. Thanksgiving, a time to be thankful. Christmas a time of joy and giving, and New Year's Day a new beginning with fresh dreams and hopes. None of that was true for me. I didn't know how to live without my mother. I was inclined to hide my feelings and to make everyone believe at school and with neighbors and family, that I was doing alright. *Everything is just fine!* It was the 70's, and therapy for adolescents didn't take up much space in our yellow pages. Besides, we were taught from the school of Tough it Out. I began to realize that you never stop missing your mom, you just get used to the constant pain.

One of the hardest obstacles was listening to my dad, late at night sobbing. My dad, who was Authority, Respect, and a looming Presence, cried like a child. I guess it shouldn't have come as a surprise that soon after that, he came home with a 'special friend' he wanted me to meet. Okay, I may have been only fourteen, but something told me this was more than a friend, and that she wasn't going to be mine.

Four months later they were married. It probably wasn't her fault, but I just couldn't bring myself to call her mom, to see all my mother's things being replaced by her flashy counterfeits, and to see my father mesmerized by her female charms. Somewhere around that time I started getting tired of the pitying glances I got from my friends from school and started spending more time with friends that were more fun, didn't know my past, and didn't really care.

I was introduced to alcohol, and took pleasure in the way those fancy little flowered cigarettes made me look older, debonair. My grades started falling drastically, and I thought myself pretty clever to tell my guidance counselor that I was still suffering from my mother's death, which the excused absences allowed me more time to chum with the crowd that didn't bother with school.

At sixteen my father bought me a new car, and several months later my license was revoked for getting a DUI. My dad, the man I had respected, admired, and secretly feared, became my enemy. The respect I used to feel for him vanished, which led me to talking back, sneering at his new wife, and rebelling in every way I could. I resented any form of authority. Unfortunately for me, my step-mother found my actions too unnerving, and I found myself out on the streets with no place to go.

That is where I found out firsthand what the birds and bees were all about. Without a place to live, and feeling smug and rebellious, I landed with an older guy, who had a dazzling smile and walking ego. He was a smooth talker, and had this young girl enamored and thinking he loved me. Not bothering to let my siblings know where I was, my life became one narcissistic act after another. I fancied myself in love, but sadly, I had found love in all the wrong places, and for all the wrong reasons.

# Chapter 3

Bobby taught me a lot about love, like how to treat "your old lady" like yesterdays newspaper. I never did quite understand how I could be the old lady when I was eight years younger than him. He also taught me about night life, and drugs, and things that I would squeeze shut my eyes and hope my mother couldn't see me, wherever she might be. There were many nights when I thought the living room was a miniature Woodstock, and I soon knew what a week long high was all about. Drug deals came and went during all hours of the night. Life became one empty thrill after another.

My sisters caught up with me in the same hospital I had gone with Mrs. Kirkland only a few years earlier, with something they labeled as a breakdown. It was tough looking at my sisters who had shown me kindness, knowing I wasn't the same girl they last saw. The mirror reflected a hardened face, an empty heart and a mental vacuum that fell into a tangled tumbling mess of vivid memories, of happier innocent times. I vowed then that I would change, clean up, and quit the life that was dragging me down and making me into someone I didn't like or understand.

"Come home with me," Katie whispered forgiveness in her voice. "Come home and you can heal. I will take care of you, sweetie. Everything will be alright."

Without too much hesitation, I agreed, knowing without some sense of an anchor, I would drown. Katie tried hard to make her apartment a refuge for me. I found a job working at a factory making meager pay. The days were long, but the nights were longer. And as much as I talked myself into remembering what a jerk Bobby was, I couldn't help but remember the times that were wild, crazy and fun. Katie tried her best to invoke into me a sense of right and wrong. There was goodness in her and Shelley that wasn't in me. But in my eyes, right was boring and wrong was fun. So I quit my job, left the safe haven, and headed back to the dark side.

Bobby welcomed me back into his den of poison, until he found me for the second morning in a row retching over the toilet, holding my hair back, and sobbing, No sense in trying to convince myself or Bobby into believing this was a result from a morning after hangover.

"Baby, this isn't something you get over, ok?" Bobby scoffed, "and you aren't going to get better. You're pregnant, and you're an idiot for not being more careful."

He rammed his fists into his pockets, and his jaw tightened. "You can't stay here anymore. You are more trouble than you're worth. Go on. You can come back when you have things taken care of."

"No! You can't talk to me like that." I stammered. Confirming the obvious, I mentally calculated the last time I had my period. Panic started working its icy fingers up to my throat while my stomach betrayed me again. "Bobby, please don't get mad at me. We love each other, right? You don't know for sure. Let me figure something out. Don't do this! I thought you loved me."

"Hey, baby, don't get too stuck on yourself. You're okay, but you're not that great to ruin my life over."

I struggled to put on a face that I hoped would say, "This doesn't hurt. My world isn't falling apart. You mean nothing to me, and this baby inside of me doesn't matter."

I held that expression for as long as it took to slam the door, and then my world did fall apart, shattering into tiny broken pieces.

Have you ever felt that empty hole inside that screams you are a loser, no one cares about you, and girl, you *are* all alone? What was it that Mrs. Kirkland had told me that night on the way home from the hospital? Something about God would take care of me or help me through this. Ha! So, God where are you? Probably taking care of someone much more deserving than me.

So, it's just me. Me to figure out a solution to this mess I'm in. Alright, I can't go to my dad. My sisters would be so disappointed in me. I tried to picture myself with a baby, then my mind would go to "taking care of things" like Bobby suggested. I thought of myself nine months pregnant and then thought of just getting rid of the problem. How would it feel to have a little one who needs me and someone I could call my own? Or how would it feel to get this confusion over with and gone in an afternoon? Well, it wouldn't hurt to just find out about "it". After all, having a baby didn't just mean nine months of being pregnant, but a whole life of sacrifices and any thought of living with Bobby again down the drain. It wasn't, after all, a being. It was just a mass of nothing. Better get rid of it. I wasn't mother material.

# Chapter 4

Something inside a person changes when choices are made that carves into the human soul. A bitterness and hardness took over as I found myself stoically waiting in a room with cold plastic chairs, giving my life over to the fates. There had been some crazy religious people on the sidewalk when I entered the building that promised a solution, with signs I ignored, and somewhere I had heard myself shout, "Shut up. Get a life." What a bunch of zealous bigots who had no idea what I was going through. Maybe their God took care of them. Maybe their God didn't take their mother away from them when they needed her most.

It was 1976, and the controversial Roe v. Wade 's historic Supreme Court decision that overturned a Texas interpretation of abortion law and making abortion legal in the United States had happened three years earlier. Lucky for me. But the debate continued with those who called themselves pro choice, and those on the other side who fiercely fought for life.

Well, I needed a cigarette badly, and as soon as this was over I could go on a week long high. But first, get this over with. After seeing a nurse with all the care and concern of an earthworm, she explained all about the "procedure" and what to expect, and about the slight cramping sensation. She started reading about liability and payments, while I glanced around the sterile room and felt like I had landed in a crazy fiction story with a bad ending.

"Just let me sign the papers, or whatever I have to do." I bit my lip and silently cursed the cards I had been dealt.

"Alright, honey. Just a minute, okay? Do you have someone to drive you home?" The nurse had a crisp white uniform that reeked competence, but no compassion.

"Yes, yes, they are waiting out in the car. They didn't want to come in."

"Well, read these papers, sign here, and I assume you brought money with you." She handed me a pen, and I signed some fictitious name, and handed them back to Miss Congeniality.

*Oh, please, let's get this over with.* My stomach was churning, and I thought about what was going on in my body. A baby, or no, not a baby, just a mass right now. Not a baby. No, not a baby.

Another nurse came in, explained a few more details, then looked at me, and asked if I was sure I knew what I was doing.

"Yes!" I answered louder than I meant to. I was sent into another room where I was given a hospital gown. The next thing I was laying down in a cold sterile room and people were talking to me, and for some crazy reason all I could think of were those weirdo's outside with signs, and now in my mind, I knew what the signs said. "It's a child." "Don't make the wrong choice." "Abortion is murder." A whirring sound filled the room, and the doctor who was only a mask with gloved hands started doing things that were painful while the whirring noise kept getting louder, and the room started spinning.

"NO!" *Stop, oh please, stop.* "Please, no more. I've changed my mind."

"You can't change your mind", the mask said in a muffled voice. "We have already started."

"No, I want you to stop. Right now. I am getting out of here." To my own ears I sounded hysterical, and I must have sounded crazy enough that they did stop.

As the terrible whirring noise subsided, there was clearly a room full of medical staff that were irritated with me.

"You will be back," one nurse predicted. "You don't really have any other choice."

My thoughts were only on getting dressed and getting out of there.

When the cool spring air hit my face I was so relieved to be temporarily reprieved, that I shouted to the sign carrying nuts, "Well, you won this time!"

When I pulled up to my sister's house, I crawled into bed in a fetal position and cried myself to sleep. If it is okay to kill a baby, what's so wrong with just ending my life, too?

That happened on Wednesday. By early Sunday morning my head was burning with fever and I was throwing up every few minutes. I felt like I was dying. Well, isn't that what I was wanting a few days ago? I woke Katie, and told her something was happening and I needed to go to the hospital.

"Are you sure it isn't the flu or something?" a sleepy sister asked hopefully.

"Uh, I am pretty sure." My head was throbbing and my stomach felt like it was on fire.

Katie threw some clothes on, half carrying and half dragging me to the car. I knew there would be some explaining to do eventually. Right now I could only moan.

Somewhere on the way to the hospital I lost consciousness. I remember waking to bright lights and a kind face of a doctor, who looked more fatherly than a sterile doctor.

"Hello, there, young lady. You can be very thankful that you are still here with us. You were a very sick girl." He patted my hand.

I jerked my hand away. "I'm not thankful."

The doctor wrote something on the chart, adjusted my IV, and then pulled over a chair to sit next to me.

"I don't know if you realize it, but it is Easter morning. I am going to be heading to church now, to celebrate the resurrection of our Lord. It has been a long night, and I'm sorry to tell you that you lost your baby. You are pretty scraped up inside, and may have a hard time ever having children. But you are alive, and you will heal physically, but I think you will struggle with a lot of emotions with this and all that you have bottled up inside. I can suggest a social worker who can talk with you, and I would also personally recommend that when you get back on your feet, you might want to spend some time in church yourself."

"First of all Doc, I'm not going to church. And I don't care if I ever have children, and I don't appreciate your pious little attitude. Go ahead and go to church, and say a prayer for your evil patient you rescued from hell today." I turned my head away from his penetrating eyes, before he saw the tears rolling down on to my pillow.

My next visitors were Shelley and Katie. It was difficult to face them. By the look of their expressions, they knew everything. Well, surely they knew their little sis was no saint by now. Still, it was hard watching their pained glances, yes, even pitying looks.

For the next few days, my sisters stayed by my bed, and comforted me. In spite of trying to put on a tough exterior; they knew me enough to know I was hurting. Then on the day I was to be released, I had another visitor. Bobby.

No one could say he wasn't a good looking guy! With heart pounding, I started a mental mantra: he is a loser, he's no good, don't listen to him. But Bobby had a way of talking a mouse into the embrace of a cat. A tom cat at that. My sisters weren't swayed by his good looks, and told him where he could get off.

He filled the doorway, wearing a black tee shirt, blue jeans and a smirk. Sauntering over to my bed, giving a cursory glance at my sisters, he winked. "Hey, baby, how about some time alone. Just for a few minutes. Tell your mother hens I just want to talk to you." He pointed to my sisters with a smile that started already to rattle my resolve.

"Grace," Shelley pled, "you don't need to talk to him. You know you are welcome to come home with me or Katie. Don't even think about leaving with him. He is the reason you're here! Think this through Grace!"

"Just give me a few minutes, Shelley. I'll be fine." I heard the door quietly close and I was left with Temptation. It really is something when we can make excuses for someone's behavior, and even blame ourselves for what someone else has done wrong. I was finding myself ready to apologize to *him* for being in this stupid hospital.

Bobby looked at me with sad brown eyes. "Baby, do you know how much I've missed you? Wow, I was shocked when I heard you were in the hospital. I know I was hard on you the last time I saw you. Come back. I'm going to treat you like the queen that you are. No one cares about you like I do, baby."

With a sinking heart, I knew by my lack of resolve, that he had won. By the time Katie and Shelley came back in the room, they knew the answer, too. I left with Bobby that afternoon on a downward spiral that would eventually land me at the bottom of a miserable pit.

Drugs and alcohol to make a person happy didn't have that effect on Bobby or me. Bobby became downright mean, and I became a bitter, hard person, far from being happy. There were moments when my conscience would kick in, and I would pray to any higher power, to have mercy on me and not let my mother see what I was doing.

Somewhere along the way, Bobby went from verbal abuse to physical. Now I know better, but I was at a stage in my life when feeling bad about myself and the world in general was a way of life. Maybe you've never been there before, but feeling like a loser, I believed that this is what I deserved. The truth is, when I would look in the mirror, I not only saw a loser, but someone that just didn't care anymore. And then I would think that Bobby was the best that I could do.

Time was elusive and vague, and I'm not sure how long I stayed with Bobby, but there were other Bobby's out there that I seemed to attract like bees to honey . . . sour honey. I found myself in jail a couple of times, once for possession and once for being at the wrong place with the wrong crowd. As bad as jail was, sometimes it was just a relief to get out of my life, and hang out with women of like kind, and three meals a day. My sisters never gave up on me, and not only bailed me out of jail, but also offered to bale me out of the sinking ship of a life.

# Chapter 5

It seems I had a cousin that lived in Park City, Utah, that was willing to take me in. Trying to inspire me, Shelley described a cozy log cabin, nestled in pine trees at an altitude of 7200 feet. Trying to remember geography in high school, I couldn't even think where Utah might be. But wherever it was, it couldn't be far enough or high enough to run from my problems. Before I knew it, I was slumped down on a seat and looking out the window of a Greyhound bus headed for the vast mysterious west. If anyone would have bothered to see me, they would have seen a very frightened, and confused young woman, cleverly disguised with a scowl and look that said *don't mess with me*! The bus ride seemed to go on forever, stopping frequently at stops along the way. The plains of Nebraska turned into craggy mountains of Wyoming. I was struck by the blue sky and yellow wildflowers of June that spotted the sides of the highway, and the miles of open spaces in between each stop. I thought of a poem my mother had taught me as a little girl that went something like:

*And what is so rare as a day in June?*
*Then, if ever, come perfect days;*
*Then Heaven tries the earth if it be in tune,*
*And over it softly her warm ear lays:*
*Whether we look, or whether we listen,*
*We hear life murmur, or see it glisten*

And another part flitted through my mind . . .

*Joy comes, grief goes, we know not how;*
*Everything is happy now,*
*Everything is upward striving;*
*'Tis as easy now for the heart to be true*
*As for grass to be green or skies to be blue,*
*'Tis for the natural way of living:*

*Oh, mama! If only you hadn't gone. If only I was sitting by your side, knowing that same joy and happiness that was there in my childhood living room, knowing how much you loved me. Remember how you would stroke my hair as you read in that lilting rhythmic voice? Do you see me? Do you know how lonely and afraid I am?*

In Rock Springs we picked up a couple more passengers. As we all got out to stretch and use the bathroom, I noticed one was a woman in her late sixties dressed in purple from her cowboy hat to her boots. A rodeo queen in her day, I surmised. The other was a young man, hard to guess his age, as his body bore the ravages of a drug addict. Before turning my gaze away, he caught my eye and shuffled over to me.

"Hey, Blondie. Can I bum a cigarette from ya?"

"I only have two left." He made me uneasy standing so close to me. I could smell his stale breath and unwashed body.

"Perfect," he grinned revealing decayed teeth. "One for me and one for you."

"Fine. Here you go." I started heading back toward the bus.

"Blondie, I need a light."

Sighing, I fished through my purse and pulled out a Bic lighter. "Keep it."

I settled in my seat next to the window. In its reflection, I saw the same guy sitting down next to me.

"I'd rather you didn't sit here."

"My name is Poe. What's yours Blondie?"

Grabbing my purse I finagled my way around him, and headed to the front of the bus.

"Sir," I tried to get the attention of the bus driver. "Sir, there is man back there that is bothering me. Could you please tell him to move?"

"These ain't assigned seats, lady."

Making a disgusted face, I started heading back down the aisle. By then most of the seats were filled up. I chose an aisle seat next to a man who had slept through the bus stop, and was taking up half of my seat. *Anything is better than sitting next to that nut case.* Poe was up three rows on the right. He swung his head around and started chattering again.

"People like you look down your nose at people like me. But the funny thing is, nobody plans on landing where I am. Too many highs, Blondie, take you down to lower levels than you ever meant to go."

I stared out the window, trying to ignore him. "I bother you because you know you might end up like me one of these days. Oh, you think you are better and stronger than that. But someday you might be on a bus watching people move away from you." He waved his arm in a big circle that encompassed the whole bus. With a raised voiced he continued his ranting. "Anyone on this bus could be sitting in my seat." He punched the air with his finger for emphasis. "Any one of you." Looking back at me, he gave me a demonic grin then slumped back in his chair. The only positive thing I could think of was I was getting off at the next stop.

I hadn't seen my cousin Melody since my mother's funeral. Since that time was such a blur, I don't remember even talking to her. I do remember fun times as young girls, though. She was a few years older than I was, making her about twenty-six now. Melody had always been athletic, and had a contagious laugh. We used to swim at Goshorn Lake in Michigan during our yearly summer reunions. Now she had moved out West to ski, and of course the last six or seven years of my life, had been spent in a hell of my own making, far removed from the carefree days of adolescence.

After being cooped up in a swaying bus with crazy people, we finally pulled into the Salt Lake City bus terminal early afternoon on a Thursday. There was Melody with her big smile, waving her arm like a flag in a hurricane. As soon as I saw her I was struck by two things; she had enthusiasm and a deep down joy. Two things I did not possess. I felt like I was the older cousin, weighed down by life and bitterness.

It truly was a relief that she was there. What in the world would I have done left alone in this strange city? I started bracing myself for whatever lay ahead. The mountains were amazing, I had to admit. They surrounded the whole city, rising up out of the flats of the Salt Lake Valley like rocky giants. The open sky revealed a whole new palette of blues.

"Grace! It is so good to see you! How was the trip? What do you think of Utah? Wait until you see Park City. It is so gorgeous. Do you have any more bags? Do you need help carrying anything? Oh, Grace, you look so tired. Let's get you home, and you will feel better."

I was somewhat overwhelmed by her exuberance. And the bit about going *home*? Where home really was, I wasn't sure, but it definitely wasn't here. This was just a dumping ground until I figured my way out of this mess called life.

"It's good to see you too, Melody. And I am pretty tired. Thanks for picking me up." Melody was shorter than my five foot seven inches. Her ash blonde hair was cut short, formed perfectly around her animated pixie face; brown expressive eyes that seemed to embrace life with vitality.

We headed to a beat up old VW Bug, Melody dragging suitcases, and me trying to keep up with my overzealous cousin. Heading up I-80, I was struck again at the majesty of the mountains and the bluest sky I had ever seen. I started wishing I could be as, well, the best word I could think of, was *free*, as my cousin was. I could feel Melody glance over at me a few times with a look of concern etched on her face. Okay, I know the last few years hadn't helped me win any beauty contest, but hey, the tightness in my chest, and the clenching of my jaw seemed to be my way of living. I was tired. Tired of life, tired of the choices I had made, tired of shoving into the back cave of my mind the child that had been conceived and that was no longer here, and tired of the bitterness that clung to me like a sour stench.

A half hour later, Melody pulled onto a gravel driveway that led to a cabin looking place. It could have been professionally craned in and dropped in the middle of a pine tree forest. A story book picture of Hansel and Gretel crept into my mind. If it wasn't for wanting a cigarette really bad, and maybe a stiff drink, I could have almost smiled at the craziness of this little place in the middle of nowhere. Inside the high ceilings that were buttressed with strong wood beams greeted me. Stacked firewood lay next to a rock fireplace. On top of the mantle ticked an old school house clock.

"So, what do you think, Grace? You are going to love it here. There are hummingbirds, and all kinds of wildlife, like deer, and elk, and even moose that come up that trail right by the house. Yesterday we saw a full rainbow that was simply amazing. You really can see the hand of God in everything, not to mention the fresh clean mountain air."

*God? Amazing? Right . . .*

I watched a wasp dance furiously on the windowpane. I felt a headache mushrooming inside of my head. Somehow being near Melody made my own life look even more messed up.

"Let me show you the house." Melody grabbed my hand, and starting pulling me through the house upstairs and down.

"This is a pretty big house for just you, isn't it?" Melody had fixed the cabin up with rustic décor. It seemed there were moose accents everywhere. In the bedroom that she labeled as "my room" was a plaque that read: Faith is the substance of things hoped for, and the evidence of things not seen." I assumed it was some Bible verse. Oh please don't tell me my cousin is some kind of religious nut. Did I remember any parties with Melody? None that I could recall. Great. Just so she doesn't start preaching at me.

"Well, in the winter, I rent all these rooms out at a pretty good price. Park City is a big ski town, and rooms are at a premium then." She smiled and added, "But don't you worry about this winter. Right now we are going to enjoy a great summer together. I work the breakfast and lunch crowd at Mt. Air Café, and have evenings and weekends off. Then in the winter, I am a ski instructor. I can't wait to teach you how to ski! If you want, we could talk to my boss at the café, and see if you could get a job waiting tables with me. We'd have a blast."

Melody's jovial chatter was too much.

"Grace? What's up with you? Where are you going?" Melody watched as I headed to the front door.

Unlatching it, I mimicked, "Oh, just going out for a walk and maybe yell at a few deer or moose or whatever those weird looking things are called. Listen, Melody. It's not you. I just have a lot on my mind, and as you can tell, the last few years haven't' been too kind to me. I'm just going to walk to the store. I'll be back."

Melody bent her head back and let out a full bellied laugh. "So, where are you walking to? The nearest store is about six or seven miles away. Come on Grace. Just relax and get settled. We have a lot to catch up on. We can go to the store after dinner. I can't wait to show you around Park City. Then we can start making plans!"

I uttered a groan, visualizing this cozy little cabin growing prison bars on the window. "Melody, I do appreciate you letting me stay here. I'm not going to stay here long, okay? I know you have your life, and work, and whatever you do, and I don't want to get in your way. I'm not the same person you remember me being. You and I are miles apart right now. You never lost your mom, and your father never deserted you. You don't know what I have been through. You have a nice easy life here, and I am happy for you."

Melody exhaled loudly, got up off the couch and went into the kitchen. I soon heard pots and pans clanking, and cupboards being opened and slammed shut. Ah! So she isn't little Miss Cheerful all the time. Well, at least we got some things laid out. I leaned against the kitchen door frame, "Melody, I can help with dinners. Just don't get any big ideas about making me be like you. I'm not."

Melody whipped around, and shoved her hands in her pockets. "Grace, you really haven't a clue do you? Everyone has problems, many worse than you. But you have an attitude, girl, that you are going to have to shed. Maybe you are only going to stay here a few days, if that's what you want. But in those few days, you are going to have to think of something or someone besides poor Grace."

# Chapter 6

The first full day at the cabin in the woods taught me what cabin fever feels like. I was restless most of the night. Somewhere I fell asleep, because I had a dream that left me shaken. At the beginning of the dream I was running and sometimes skipping through a field of blue and yellow flowers. I knew I was an adult, but it felt as if I was a young child, without fears or worry. Up ahead, I saw a stream of light coming down from azure skies. There was such a yearning to reach that ray of light and stand in it. As I neared the light, I felt a soft mist on my face and body and a fragrance I couldn't describe, except that it made me happy. It seemed within a moment's time the clouds got dark and ominous. Behind me a heard laughter, clearly not a joyful sound, but laced with menace. Bobby was running toward me, and as he stepped on each flower they wilted in his wake. A sense of panic reared in my being as I was torn between leaving the glorious shaft of light, or of being caught in Bobby's grasp. As I saw him getting closer and closer, he smiled revealing blackened teeth. Screaming in horror, I woke with my chest thundering, and sweat running down my temples. I stayed awake to watch as morning painted the sky violet than mauve. Strange how some dreams stay with you with full color clarity, while others are barely remembered.

Shuffling around the house, I wondered what I could possibly find to do here. A glass of orange juice, and a bowl set out for cereal were on the counter. Melody had written a note telling me to make myself at home, and to have a good day. The phone sat near her note, silently in its cradle which beckoned me with the crazy desire to call Bobby of all people. What would he think of me way out in Utah? Did he ever think of me? I knew he was danger, but it beat sitting here doing nothing. I realized calling long distance wasn't really fair to Melody, but who cares? I wasn't going to stay here for long anyway. I called long distance information, and lo and behold, the same number from years ago, came back to me through the operator. Well, he hasn't landed too far, I chuckled.

I quickly dialed his number before I changed my mind.

"Yeah! Hello!" At the sound of his voice, my heart started beating like a kettle drum.

"Hey, Bobby, guess who this is?" I hated hearing the quiver in my voice.

"Gracie? Hey, baby, I'd know that voice anywhere! Whatcha doing?" He could have been in the next room; he seemed so close, like the last four years apart hadn't happened.

"Well, I'm in Utah! Can you believe that? I, well, I'm kind of trying to get my life figured out."

"Oh, yeah? Well, we had life pretty figured out, didn't we baby?"

Oh, man. What was I doing? What possessed me to call this guy? My hands felt clammy holding the phone. I ought to hang up.

"How are you and everybody? Anything new?"

"Oh, just messing around. And you?"

"I'm okay. Hanging in there. Well, Bobby, I better get off the phone. It's my cousin's phone, and I better not run up the long distance bill. Just wanted to say hi."

There was a poignant silence, and then in that same sultry voice I remembered too well, he whispered, "I've missed you, Gracie. You can come back home anytime."

No cigarettes, no anything in this house in the middle of nowhere. I paced the floor, opened cupboards, turned on the TV, turned it off again, and felt like screaming. I could call my sisters and ask for money to come back home. And then what?

# Chapter 7

Brad shouldered open the back screen door as he carried out a plate with two fine looking T-bone steaks on it. Not wanting to miss out, Maggie, his old faithful black Lab, followed close at his heels. After slapping the steaks onto the well-used grill and adding some spices, Brad picked up an old squeak toy and gave it a throw. Maggie, a bit overweight, but with full Retriever instincts, chased after the toy and dropped it at her hero's feet, ready and poised for the next throw. Brad gauged in his mind how long it would take to grill the steaks to medium rare perfection, before he needed to heat up a can of pork and beans and butter some bread to complete a hungry man's bachelor dinner. Okay, maybe not the healthiest meal, but right now it would satisfy the hollow spot groaning in his stomach. It was hard to miss Brad in a crowd. He was tall, dark brown hair, patriarch nose, square jaw, and broad shoulders.

Hurling the slobbered on purple cow for Maggie, he sat down and thought of how his life had changed since he had filled the hollowness in his heart with a relationship with Jesus Christ. Growing up in a small rural farm community in the Midwest, with five siblings, Brad didn't have much time to contemplate life, death or any other churchy subject. Brad had never known his father. He had left sometime after the sixth child had been born, leaving his mother without money, or a car, but a determination to raise her kids with at least a lot of love. Needless to say, Brad Halverson and his brothers and sister were often out running and cajoling other neighborhood kids to join in their rowdiness. Brad was caught up in the sex, drugs and rock and roll revolution, but found out quick enough that girls got him in trouble, drugs made him stupid, and rock and roll hurt his hearing. He observed many of his peers going down the slippery slide of drugs into destruction. It seemed that not many crawled back up, unless they had some help from a superior force. So on one of those muggy summer nights, when the shirt clung to your back and life seemed to slow down to a crawl, Brad and his best bud Randy found their way to a good old fashioned revival meeting. Arming themselves with firecrackers and booze, they made their way into the circus looking tent.

Randy was all for sitting up front, to get the best bang for his buck. People were filing in from every direction to the sound of organ playing. Brad recognized some folks, but many must have come in from all parts of the county.

"Maybe we better sit in the back, Randy. I know some of these people! That way we can make a quick escape when we start firing up this old joint."

We had a good old time poking fun at the preacher who was already sweating in his three piece suit, and the organist lady who would get so excited at all the people coming in, she would forget the chords. The more Randy and I tipped our little silver flask, the funnier everything got. Then a hush permeated the room, as the preacher man stood up, lifted his Bible up to the sky and with feeling declared, "We will now pray!"

The rest of the night didn't go at all like Brad or Randy had planned. When that old preacher got to swaying and working up about judgment and grace, and love and mercy, heaven and hell, well, those two boys found themselves on the edge of their seats, firecrackers forgotten. Both nearly jumped out of their seats when the organist broke into an altar call song, and the preacher begged sinners to come home. Brad watched as people in all shapes and sizes, old and young streamed to the front, tears mingled with joy.

"Lets' get out of here," Randy whispered. "This is creepy."

Brad wasn't sure about the word *creepy* but something strange was sure going on. The next night they found themselves entering that old tent, and this time working their way up to the front, minus firecrackers and flask.

Brad couldn't really remember all that the preacher said that next night, but he did remember the part about a caring, loving Potter and the clay. It wasn't a unique concept, since the preacher said it came straight from the Bible.

But the part that God cared about him, a lump of clay, a wild and reckless teenager, cared enough to want to make something beautiful and useful out of his life, was what started him delving deeper with his thinking. A relationship with the God of the universe? Now that was something. The preacher made it so personal. Something about God loving him so much that He sent His own son to die for him. To take away his guilt and shame. And he had that, for sure! How God's message to man is not condemnation. His message to man is, "Come, come; the salvation of God is available to all." Something was moving in his heart, and as he and Randy made their way to the tent for the third night, he found out it was the Spirit of God working in his heart. And when that old organist started the altar call, he found himself moving to the front with others. It really wasn't explainable, but it gave him a peace in his heart, and amazement as he looked beside him and saw his rough and ready friend next to him with tears sliding down his face.

Because they were both very much male teenagers, neither one of them spoke on the way home of what had happened. In some ways it was a little embarrassing to think about what had just transpired, but for the next few years until graduation, Randy and Brad had a bond deeper than any friendship; it was the bond of brotherhood that only comes through the blood of Christ.

After graduation, Randy went away to college on the East coast, and Brad decided to head out West to California. Somewhere outside of Evanston, Wyoming, he fell in love with a sleepy little mountain town, called Park City. Park City had been founded in 1870 as a mining community, and actually once was the site of the largest silver-mining camp in the country. The first ski resort, called Treasure Mountain, opened in 1963. There was quite a migration of young people heading west like Brad, who became attracted to the greatest snow on earth with the dry climate and massive Rocky Mountains making for great skiing.

Brad rolled into town in early fall, and was in awe of the Aspen trees in their full golden glory. He rented out a small bedroom that was part of an original miners shack on the main street of town. Although it had been renovated, it clearly held to Brad the historical fascination of an era gone by. At that time Park City was best described as a wild and bawdy mining town known for its saloons and houses of prostitution. He often imagined what life must have been like for a silver miner. Sometimes more than a mile underground, the miner had only a head lamp to illuminate his way through the dark and dusty tunnel. Spending his day drilling, blasting, and mucking, he would work underground for ten hours a day, four days a week.

Brad was able to get a job at a local sporting goods store, where his co-workers helped him catch the fever of skiing, not so unlike the predecessors in his shack may have felt over mining for silver. He signed up for night classes at a small community college in Salt Lake. He also found out that winters come early in the Rocky Mountains.

# Chapter 8

Melody came home after work about 3:00 pm with a friend she introduced as Carmen Sanchez. Carmen had a pretty face, but even more appealing was her quick smile and gentle spirit. I learned that Melody and Carmen worked together at Mt. Air, and according to Melody, "they kept each other sane."

"Oh, yes," Carmen grinned, "there are some crazy people come in there!"

"Did you have a good day, Grace?" Melody was already flying about the kitchen throwing together what looked like a roast, with carrots and potatoes and onions.

"This is my mother's recipe, Grace. "Since our mother's were sisters, I bet your mother has made this same pot roast for you."

It had been quite a while since I had a good home cooked meal, let alone one that I could practically taste from the past. It was kind of Melody to think of me. But this wasn't my home, and it wasn't my mother cooking this meal, and I felt like a complete stranger without a clue what I was doing.

"What did you do today, Grace?" Melody and Carmen looked so domestic as they laughed and giggled over how the cook had run out of eggs for breakfast and had put up a sign on the chalkboard that read, "The hens went on strike, try the pancake special."

"Well, not much. Couldn't find much to do," I whined

"Great, because Monday you can go with me to work, and see if you can't take Carmen's place as a breakfast and lunch server. Because, our Miss Carmen here, has been promoted to night shift which makes a lot more tip money."

"I can't do that, Melody. First, I am only staying for a few days. Second, I have never waited on tables, and don't plan on starting. Ever."

"Oh, Grace. Just humor me. It would be fun working together. I will be missing Carmen so much, that I will need my cuz there to be my friend!"

"Yeah, well, I can just see me there on the interview saying something like, I'm sure you would want to hire me since I have absolutely no experience, and I will only be here one more day." Clearly Melody wasn't thinking straight.

"Just think about it over the weekend, Grace. Tomorrow you and I are going on a hike. You are going to love all the spectacular trails here."

"Uh, I doubt that. I'm not really into hiking." What did she think I looked like? I definitely wasn't the hiking outdoor girl that she was. If she thought she could push me into things I didn't want to do, she was wrong. I might even be gone by Monday.

That night we three sat down to the pot roast meal. I was appalled when Carmen and Melody grabbed my hand to pray. But what really disturbed me was the way Melody prayed as if God was really listening, and even crazier, that He would care. Then Melody started praying about me.

"Lord, thank you so much that Grace can be here. I know you have a plan for her life. I know she has been down a rough road, but You promised that if we acknowledge You, then You will direct our paths. Help her to see how very much You love her. In Jesus Name, Amen"

I was so stunned at her prayer that I didn't know what to say, or why my eyes were filling up. It just seemed so bizarre. How can these seemingly normal people think that God was listening? And if there was a God, then He also would know who I am, and that I wasn't worth caring about, and certainly not worth praying for.

As I sat there bewildered, Melody started dishing out carrots, potatoes, and onions. She forked a generous slab of meat on our plates, with a hot roll.

"This is a symphony of my taste buds," Carmen smiled. "Delicious."

"Oh, definitely Mozart," Melody laughed.

*And mom*, I thought, as just the exact seasonings brought me back home.

I woke up the next morning to an impossible cheerful voice chirping, "Graaaacce, time to get uuuppp."

Last night sleep evaded me, as I was completely sober and without nicotine or anything that would coax me into a stupor. I hated being so clear headed, and the mountain air I think, was getting to my brain. I wanted so desperately to escape, but where was I supposed to go? I felt trapped, and in this sober state, felt like a deep hunger that was driving me nuts. The strange part was that the hollow emptiness didn't seem to be derived from any addiction, but from an even deeper hunger, I couldn't figure out.

Now here it was morning already, and my overly jovial jail keeper was making coffee and pancakes in preparation for the big hike ahead. Could I plead sickness? If I ignore her, will she just go away? Even in the summer, the morning sun peeked over chilly mountain tops, warming frost from grassy tips. I had to admit it was beautiful, but I had become a night person over the years, and this was torture.

We headed out straight from the house and started a climb that left me digging deep into my lungs to get some breath. Melody had loaned me some hiking boots and a back pack, and I couldn't help but envision how my friends back home would be laughing at my attire. "Melody, this is not my idea of fun. I can hardly breathe. Do you think I am some kind of a mountain goat?"

Melody exhaled, "You can't breathe because you have smoked too much, and we are at a pretty high elevation compared to your home. Now take a big sip of water, and try to enjoy the beauty around you for a change."

"I haven't smoked anything in days. And to tell you the truth, I really am not digging all this health stuff."

"Actually, this is a fairly easy hike. I'm starting you off easy, but by the end of the summer you will be racing right past me on some serious climbs. You start breathing in clean mountain air, you won't have to keep huffing and puffing like an old buffalo."

"Melody, this is not my life. You can do whatever you want to do, but I'm not you."

Melody turned and faced me, and sighed, "Do you want to stay in the pit forever, Grace? You feel like you are safer by staying in the pit, but only true security is found in God. Yeah, I know you want to respond to that remark pretty badly, but don't bother. Come on, let's go a little farther. There is a gorgeous meadow up ahead, with a riot of wildflowers. It will give you a heady joy that no Jim Beam or dope can give you."

Well, the truth is that I did sleep soundly that night. Carmen had come over in the afternoon. I envied the easy way the two friends chatted and laughed in an easy banter. I definitely was the outsider looking in. It had been a long time since I had a friend that I could laugh and joke with so effortlessly. I started making plans to call Katie or Shelley in the morning, and ask them to send some money so I could leave here. Maybe they were tired of bailing me out of trouble all the time, picking me up each time I fell. But this Wild West wasn't my type of wild. I had overheard Melody and Carmen talking about church in the morning. That would be a good time to place the call.

But unbelievably, I heard again the crazily joyful voice hollering, "Graaaacce, time to get uuuppp."

Snarling, I barked back, "I am not getting up, and I am not going to church."

Surprisingly, after awhile I heard the front door close and all was quiet. At least she is getting the hint, I grumbled. Scrounging around the kitchen, I found coffee brewed, and homemade blueberry muffins still faintly warm from the oven, laid out on the counter. A heavy fog of melancholy settled over me. Munching on the muffin, I evaluated what Melody had told me the day before about me wanting to stay in the pit. What pit? Maybe she was the one in the pit. Maybe she was digging her own pit with all her religion. Wasn't religion just a crutch? Everyone has their thing. Mine just didn't happen to be going to church and wearing a plastered grin all the time. At least I was real.

I dialed Shelley first, and just listened to the phone keep ringing. Katie was home.

"Hey, Katie. It's Grace. How ya doing?"

"Oh, sweetie. It's so good to hear your voice. How do you like Park City?"

"Well, I don't really. I just miss everyone back there. I really want to come back. And I would in a second if I only had the money for the bus fare."

A deep sigh was followed by, "Grace, you haven't given it a chance. Aren't you getting along with Melody?"

"Oh, sure, she's really nice, but Katie, this isn't for me out here. I don't know anyone. It's just all so strange. Please help me out."

For a minute I thought our connection was lost, and then she replied slowly, "Grace, even if I had the money, I think you need to stay there awhile. You need to get your head straightened out. Get away from your friends here."

"Oh, so it's my big bad friends you don't like. Well, thanks, sis. Maybe Shelley will be nicer to me."

"You can try calling her, Grace, but I know she feels the same way as I do. I'm sorry you are so miserable. Why don't you try taking a mountain hike, breathe in some fresh air? I hear it is beautiful out there."

"This is ridiculous! I feel like I'm in prison here. And nobody cares. Nobody has ever cared. I'll just figure it out without you or Shelley or anyone else. And I hate hearing about the fresh mountain air!" I slammed the phone down.

Roaming around the house, I found a notebook of Melody's with quotes from C.S. Lewis. Not sure who he was or is, I read some:

*"To be a Christian means to forgive the inexcusable because God has forgiven the inexcusable in you."*

*"He died not for men, but for each man. If each man had been the only man made, He would have done no less."*

The point of this quote struck me forcibly. Would God have died for me if I was the only person on earth? Hard to believe!

*"It would seem that Our Lord finds our desires not too strong, but too weak. We are half-hearted creatures, fooling about with drink and sex and ambition when infinite joy is offered us, like an ignorant child who wants to go on making mud pies in a slum because he cannot imagine what is meant by the offer of a holiday at the sea. We are far too easily pleased."*

*"God allows us to experience the low points of life in order to teach us lessons that we could learn in no other way."*

*"I think that if God forgives us we must forgive ourselves. Otherwise, it is almost like setting up ourselves as a higher tribunal than Him."*

*"The great thing to remember is that though our feelings come and go God's love for us does not."*

Because Melody was so different than I was, I re-read the quotes, trying to understand. As I flipped through her notebook, I found her own personal thoughts, and as I continued to skim it, I found my name.

*"My heart breaks for my cousin. She seems so empty and lost, without hope. Sometimes I just want to hold her and comfort her as I would a child, and sometimes I want to strangle her. She is so caught up in her own misery, that she can't see anything else. I pray that I will be able to draw her out of herself, and into the marvelous Light."*

Slamming the book shut, I hollered out loud, "Who does she think she is? She feels sorry for me? Her heart is breaking for me? Ha! I feel sorry for her! Miss Perfect who doesn't have a clue what real fun is. She probably has never known what it's like to be with a guy. She can save her prayers. If I was a praying woman, I would pray for her!"

Pacing back and forth, I madly tried to figure out how I could find the money to get back home. If all else failed, I could always hitch hike. Where there's a will there's a way!

When Melody came home from church, I ignored her completely. I stayed in my room with the door closed. A visual image implanted in my mind of Melody praying over her lost and hopeless cousin. Well, she would find out by Monday that I would be gone.

A little later, there was a soft knock on my door. "Grace, can I come in? I want to apologize." The door slowly squeaked open, and Melody's face peeked through the opening. "I haven't been sympathetic at all, Grace. I have been critical and judgmental. You're right. I don't know what it is like to lose a mom, or feel rejected by your dad."

I turned my face away from her and cringed. *She doesn't know the half of it.* "Well, uh, thanks, Melody. Just don't keep praying about me. That is really weird."

"Well, I don't know if I can promise that, but I won't be so in your face anymore. Deal? Now, I know waiting tables may not be your thing, but I am pretty sure that if you come with me in the morning, you could start tomorrow."

"I'm not . . ." Then it hit me that this might be my way out. I would play along with this whole job thing, and maybe after a week, I would have enough money to get outta here. "Um, how early do I have to get up?"

Melody gave me a giant smile and shrugged, "Is five thirty okay?"

I gulped. Whatever it took. "Melody, I need to confess something. This morning while I was wondering around the house, I came across a notebook filled with quotes from a C.S. Lewis guy. Who is he?"

Melody looked startled at my confession of snooping, but recovered enough to tell me that, "Lewis was an atheist and converted to Christianity after reading several different books, and talking to friends who were Christians. He was quite the writer, and poet, but after his conversion he wrote Christian books. I just have always liked the way he could use words in such an insightful and heartfelt way. Why did you want to know?"

"Oh, I was just wondering. Melody, one more thing. Could you think of a better way to wake me up in the morning instead of, 'Graaaacce, time to get uuuppp'".

She gave me a lopsided grin, and impulsively wrapped her arms around me, and whispered in my ear, "We are going to be such great friends, Gracie."

A gentle tapping on my door woke me the next morning. "Yeah, I'm up," I groaned while I squinted at the clock. It was five thirty in the morning. That was more like the time I should be going to bed than getting up, but I had a plan and I was determined to make the most of this day. My long hair was a tangled mess, so as I yanked on long blonde strands, I brushed my teeth and searched for proper interview attire. Since my wardrobe was limited to T-shirts and jeans, I just grabbed the ones that were the cleanest. Well, it's not like I'm interviewing for a CEO's position or anything.

Melody looked impossibly awake in a light blue uniform, sturdy shoes, and a smile that told me she was amused at the groggy condition I was in. "Please don't tell me that I need to wake up at this time every morning," I moaned.

"Only if you get the job, cuz."

Somewhere in route, I dozed off, and was shaken awake by Melody. "Wake up, Sport. We're here." 'Here', was a small restaurant on the outside of town. Mt. Air was one of the few restaurants in town, I learned later, that served up a traditional breakfast fare, and many locals frequented it. Patting my hair, and fixing a smile on my face, Melody and I headed for the door. I was introduced to Floyd Watson, the morning manager. It seems that Melody was right. They needed a waitress, and I was told, "Go find a uniform and apron, and Melody will show you around."

There is something about the smell of bacon frying and coffee brewing that gratifies the senses. Soon I was learning how to roll napkins, abbreviate orders, make coffee, and a dozen other foreign tasks. Then came the ominous realization that I was being led to my first customer.

It was a man, a young man, with the greenest eyes I could ever remember seeing. A chiseled face, neat brown hair, and a lean physique made quite a nice package. Thankfully, Melody was standing beside me to coax me along.

"Uh, hello there. Do you want anything?" I winced at my clumsy speech, cleared my throat, and began again. "Good morning, sir.

What would you like to order?" It wasn't that he was drop dead gorgeous, but he had a rugged handsome way about him that caused me to stumble over my words.

"Good morning to you, too. Hey, Melody. Is this a friend of yours?" His sea green eyes not only made me want to dive in, but there was a kindness in them that was a rare quality from the guys I had known.

"Hi Brad. This is my cousin Grace. This is her first day, and actually you are her first customer, so go easy."

"Sure thing. I'll just have coffee, black, and two eggs over medium, wheat toast." He gave me a warm smile, and I scampered away to give the order to the cook and grab the coffee.

The rest of the day flew by and before I knew it we were on to lunch. My legs were burning with all the scrambling around, and my mind was whirling with orders and keeping up with the never ending crowd. I feverishly looked around for Melody, who was busy delivering plates of food to a family of four.

"Melody," I whispered fiercely, "I can't go on any more. I'm beat!"

"Finish up your last order, and you can call it a day. They have enough help for the lunch crowd. Will you be okay for a few hours? I'm on until two thirty."

I nearly collapsed with relief. "No problem. I'll catch up to you about two thirty then." I changed back into my old clothes, and balled up my uniform, thankful to feel normal again. In the bathroom I washed my face, and rinsed off the hectic morning. Since the restaurant was on the edge of town, and I was worn out, I hobbled over to a hotel across the street that advertised a lounge available. The cash in my pocket from tips, allowed me thoughts of having just a quick drink while I waited for Melody. It was an upscale bar, something I wasn't used to. I ordered a Jack and Coke, bought some cigarettes, and slumped into a booth where I could elevate my aching legs. The warm amber drink burned delightfully down my throat, as I felt the craziness of the day and my life, slowly melt away. Before I knew it, I had downed three drinks, and feeling pretty good. Before I knew it I felt someone patting my denim-clad knee.

"You look lonely over here all by yourself young lady." I looked up at the face that was talking, wondering when he had sat down. He reminded me of a shifty out of town salesman, out on the prowl, but he was company, and I was lonely. Being inebriated he didn't look too bad. After a few more drinks, we found ourselves in his hotel room. Oh, I know the score, but being good and drunk, nothing really seems to matter. The funny thing was, he must have been even more soused than I was, because when I woke early in the morning we were both fully dressed. Panic gripped me as I realized I never had met Melody after her shift, and in just a few minutes my shift would start again. My pounding head was wondering how in the world I could pull myself together, and explain my absence to Melody. Scrubbing my teeth with my finger and hotel bar soap, I changed into my wrinkled uniform and raked my fingers through my hair. "What a pathetic mess you are," I mumbled dismally. Without even looking at the comatose figure lying on the bed, I let myself out and faced the brightness of a new day.

As I headed across the street and saw Melody's car in the parking lot, I did feel bad. Funny thing about regret. I had stored it down so deep over the years when I had disappointed my family, friends, myself, and right now it was lodged in my throat and choking off my air. Taking a deep breath, I squared my shoulders and faced the chastisement ahead.

The familiar aroma of morning breakfast smells assaulted my nose and I nearly lost the liquid contents of my stomach from the night before. Glancing around the room, I saw Melody busy with preparation for the morning's onslaught. Floyd gave me a brief nod, with a look that said he wasn't happy with my lateness, but to jump in. Which I did. I stayed busy all morning, avoiding Melody as much as I could. Somewhere in the business of the morning, she passed me some gum. Okay, I got the hint. My first customer from yesterday was there again. I avoided meeting his eyes, too. By the end of my shift, I felt like a truck had rolled over me. Determined not to cross my cousin anymore, I sat in her car, and fell asleep.

# Chapter 9

It was Grace who took Brad's order again the following morning. Blonde hair caught up in a pony tail, with piercing blue eyes—eyes that went deep with pain. She seemed to be avoiding Brad, or else he hadn't made a very big impression on her the day before. By the look of her, he could have guessed she was trying to ride out a hangover. He had spent enough time with *that* type of a girl. That's not what he was pursuing. Of course he had no idea if he would ever see her again, but for some crazy reason he was already looking forward to coming for breakfast again tomorrow. In the many conversations with God, Brad had become convinced that He would let him know who the right girl was. She would definitely be a Christian who loved the Lord as much as he did, and who would someday be the mother of his children—instilling godly values and morals into their lives. Brad was pretty sure that Grace wasn't that woman, but frequently he would feel his mind wander back to the pony tailed waitress. She was somewhat of a mystery, but to most males, all girls are. Brad had felt ashamed at the way he had used girls in the past, treated them with less than respect prior to his conversion. Now he was determined to keep his distance because he wasn't really sure how a man was supposed to treat the opposite gender. He was comfortable hanging out with the guys; females were a different story.

With arms folded behind his head that night, he stared at the ceiling. *She's not for you, Brad. Get a grip.* Tossing from side to side, he started counting sheep. One sheep in particular was carrying a coffee mug, with blue taunting eyes.

# Chapter 10

The ride home was heavy with a profound silence. My plan was to enjoy a long shower and take a nap when we got home, but before we got past the front door, Melody turned and faced me. "Grace, I know you don't want to be here. I am beginning to not be thrilled about you being here either. But, for now, you are living in my house, and you are going to help out. I worked longer than you did today. And although you probably didn't get much sleep last night, I didn't either. I spent most of the afternoon yesterday waiting for you to show up, and the rest of the night wondering if I should call the police, and imagining you dead somewhere. You can help here with dinner and dishes, and keeping your room clean for starters. Just because you have a chip on your shoulder, doesn't excuse you from helping out. You want me to feel sorry for you, Grace? Well, I do. I feel sorry that you can only stare at your own belly button, and not see the world and needs around you." Melody's brows were drawn down in thought, "I'm here for you if you need me, Grace. The stunt you pulled yesterday hurt. The choices you are making not only hurt others, but they hurt you. Don't you ever think of anyone but yourself?"

Well, no one likes to hear that they are selfish, so I bit back with defiance. "Don't worry, Miss Perfect. I told you that as soon as I have enough for bus fare I will leave you so you won't be hurt by my poor choices anymore."

"Grace, you know very well I'm not perfect, and I am sorry if I am coming across that I think I am prefect. But I do know One that is perfect, and that helps me make better choices. I know you feel like you got a raw deal in life. Do you remember one of the quotes from C.S. Lewis? It went something like, *God allows us to experience the low points in our life to teach us lessons that we couldn't learn any other way.* I believe that God doesn't make mistakes, so some of the hard times in our lives are actually for our good."

"Are you trying to tell me that God killed my mother to make me a better person? Wow, nice try. Guess what, God, it didn't work."

"God didn't kill your mother, Grace. But He did allow it to happen for a reason that will probably be past our finite wisdom. We live in a fallen world. This isn't God's best world, but He is preparing us for a far better place. The Bible says that His ways aren't our ways. He is bigger and wiser than we could ever think or imagine. He just wants us to trust Him."

"Just so you know, Melody. I will never believe how you believe. None of what you say makes sense."

"Do you really want a God who makes total sense? Wouldn't He be just someone on our level? We can't put God in a box of our own mental capacity. We can't lay the ground rules. He is our Creator, from everlasting to everlasting."

"Stop it! I don't want to hear it, ok?" I swore under my breath as I made my way outside to the deck. Leaning over the railing, I tried to calm my agitated mind. I watched a dainty yellow butterfly flitting on the bushes below me. Taking a deep breath, I concentrated on my plan and how soon I could leave here. Obviously I had burned another bridge, and unless I said I believed her fanatical religion, I was not wanted here.

Several minutes later, Melody stood by my side, shading her eyes with her hand. "It's beautiful out here, isn't it? There is something so comforting and tranquil to me when I gaze out at the mountains, and the pine trees that were here way before I was born. Grace, I'm going out tonight. Carmen and a few other friends of mine are going to the reservoir and build a campfire. We'll roast hotdogs and marshmallows. You are invited to come. You will probably find my friends less quick to find fault than me. I know it's hard to believe, Grace, but I do care about you. You are family." A marginal smile framed her face.

"No thanks," I chirped with what I hoped sounded like nonchalance. Then with my own smile warming, "I will be too busy looking at my own belly button."

A few hours later, I heard the front door close, while I was counting out my meager tips. I had blown my first day's tips.

# Chapter 11

Brad was looking forward to a rare night out. Working full time and going to night school left him little time to enjoy any social life. He was nearing graduation to become an architect, and had been spending long nights working on design projects for his final grade. It had been hard to stay focused the past four years, but he could finally see the end in sight. Although it had been fun working at the sporting goods store, he was praying he could land a job with a local architecture firm by fall.

He looked over at Molly, all eighty-four pounds of her stretched out on and old bear rug he had bought at a second hand store, and put in his living room. He had neglected Molly with long hours at work and school. Sometimes he could get away with bringing Molly to work with him. Now he looked over at his friend, and decided she would be overjoyed for a good romp at the reservoir, and maybe he would even sneak her a hot dog or two.

Piling into his old Chevy truck, he headed for the Rockport Reservoir State Park which was about twenty minutes from his house. A big ripe watermelon was his contribution to the summer feast. Along the way he looked for the eagle nests along the road, hoping to see an eagle in flight. It made him think of the John Denver 'Rocky Mountain High' song that declares, *"You know he'd be a poorer man if he'd never saw an eagle fly."* Well, Brad knew he was rich, definitely not in earthly wealth, but blessed in ways he would have never comprehended. He loved the serenity of the mountains, and felt God's presence in His amazing creation. It was rare that he didn't encounter some wildlife on hikes, or even driving down the canyon to Salt Lake City on his way to classes. Now as he looked for an eagle he saw one in the distance soaring over Rockport. How incredible that Bald Eagles are capable of seeing fish in the water from several hundred feet above, while soaring and gliding above, knowing how difficult it is for humans to see a fish just beneath the surface of the water from only a short distance away. Something stirred in his soul as he watched the eagle make a dive and come up with a fish in his talons. Looking back to the road, he found himself on the wrong side of the road. "Alright", he grinned, "keep your mind on your driving."

Molly could smell the water and started whining with anticipation of a perfect swim on a summer night. The reservoir water never was warm, but for Molly it was perfect. Locating the cars of his friends, he parked and let the anxious Lab out of the truck. He followed the sound of laughter and the smell of a campfire. Horseshoes were already in full swing. "Hey, Brad!" Gordy yelled out. "You're just in time to play the champs." Brad had been raised on horseshoes, so he very rarely got beat. In fact, competition ran deeply in the veins of Brad Halverson. So when the group divided into two teams to play beach volleyball, it was no surprise that Brad's side won. As the sun began to fade, and stomachs were full from too many hot dogs and S'mores, Pete got out his guitar, and the group sang around the campfire. There was a comfortable camaraderie in this gathering. Looking above him at the stars peeking out and listening to the crickets fiddling, Brad felt at peace with his life and the amazing things God continually kept showing and teaching him. Molly was worn out, but she too, looked at peace with her world.

# Chapter 12

I heard the knocking on my bedroom door, and couldn't believe it was time to get up again. I never did hear Melody come home last night. But I did have time to do some thinking, and wanted to ask my cousin a question. So, as we both climbed in to the Bug, I peered over at Melody, and said, "I have a question, and it is legitimate. I'm not trying to be sarcastic or rude, I just want to know. You seem to want me to believe like you do, but why would anyone want to be a Christian? I mean, all it seems like to me, is that you guys have all these rules. Anything that is fun, you can't do. And you talk about joy and peace, when I know a lot of people who are Christians that are pretty gloomy and unhappy."

Melody's brows wrinkled in thought, as she waited a moment to answer. "Yeah, that is a good question. It really bothers me to think that's what people think about Christians. That we can't do this or can't do that. I would love it if the world knew what we can do! When Jesus was on earth, He had some pretty radical teachings. You see, there were these guys who were religious leaders of their day. They were for the most part, pious and pretty big on themselves because they followed all the rules and regulations, and even added their own rules. There was a guy back then who was proud of being one of those religious leaders. He boasted of his lineage, saying he was faultless in his legalistic righteousness. But then this guy Paul met Jesus while on his way to persecute Christians. His conversion changed everything. All of a sudden, his perfect record meant nothing. All that mattered was knowing Christ. It isn't what we do or don't do. It's believing that we need a Savior, and that Savior is Jesus Christ. You see, today, we have those same type of people, who change the amazing relationship with Christ into rules and regulations. We add in our own made up rules, hoping to make us more righteous. But Christ alone is righteous. Paul said in a book of the Bible called First Corinthians, "Everything is permissible for me—but not everything is beneficial. Everything is permissible for me—but I will not be mastered by anything." What is sad to see, are those people you are talking about that go around all day grumpy. We as Christians can have love, joy, peace, patience, kindness, goodness, faithfulness, gentleness and self-control. But we are also human beings who are tempted just like anyone else."

Scrunching up my face in intrigue, I squinted over at Melody, "I'm not really sure what you are saying, Melody. And don't get excited thinking I'm interested in Christianity. I'm just wondering why people like you and Carmen, who are attractive women, fall for all this, when you could be having fun? Instead you're wasting your life on trying to be good."

Instead of being irritated like I thought she would, Melody burst out in a resounding, good natured laugh. "Oh, Gracie, I am having fun. I have such a full life. A life is never wasted when you have a real reason and purpose to live."

"Please don't tell me that you have more fun sitting at home reading a stuffy old Bible, than you would having a blast at the bar."

"I don't need to be high or drunk to have fun. Last night I had a super time just hanging out with friends. I wish you would have come. Brad was there."

"Who's Brad?"

"You, know, your first breakfast order. The great looking guy with the green eyes?"

"Oh, yeah, him. So he is one of you guys too?"

"If you mean is he a Christian, well, yeah he is." Melody's countenance changed into a Cheshire Cat grin. "He was asking about you."

How incredibly strange that of all the places I'd been, and all the things that I have seen and done, somehow I felt an embarrassing red flush climb up my face.

# Chapter 13

Brad was beginning to see the light at the end of the tunnel. By the end of the week, he would only have two more weeks of school, and then he would graduate. But until then, he would be using every spare minute to study for finals. He was beginning to think he had been crazy to try to cram in all the rest of the necessary classes this summer, but at age 26, he was ready to jump into his career. Working his way through school and taking night classes, had slowed him down, but soon he would be a graduate and ready to embark on life as an architect.

Somewhere in life, a man starts thinking past the days of youth, to settling down. In some men, thoughts of a wife and family don't come until later, and some not at all, but lately Brad's thoughts went down that trail. He had asked Melody about her cousin, and found out that she was not a believer. So he was determined to put her out of his head, but the more Brad forced himself not to think of Grace, the stronger the urge became.

This morning at breakfast, Brad brought his notes to study. With his mind buried in numbers and calculations, he didn't hear Grace approach.

"Let's see, eggs over medium, wheat toast, and black coffee. Am I right?" Grace was wearing a rare smile, which changed her whole countenance.

"How boring and predictable I must seem. How about this morning I change that to pancakes and bacon? But not to get too far off the norm, I'll still order my coffee black."

"Okay, you got it." She whisked off to grab the coffee, and place the order. Brad went back to his notes, and watched everything he had written down turn into a haunting face, with startling blue eyes.

"Here you go. Coffee, black, and your pancakes will be up shortly."

Since concentrating on his drawings and notes was out of the question, he recalled last night's phone call. His old pal Randy had called, and surprised him by informing Brad that he had been offered an exceptional job in Salt Lake. Although the two friends hadn't verbally interacted over the years, Randy wasn't ever far from his mind. The experience the two had shared years before, would always keep them kindred spirits. Randy would be arriving the day after Brad's graduation. Two stellar events in his life, called for a celebration. Brad began mentally planning a get together where Brad could introduce Randy to his friends, and also rejoice in being a full fledged architect. Without hesitation, Grace entered his thoughts of someone who he could invite. Out of the corner of his eye, he saw Melody and Grace hover by the coffee makers. Melody could be his inside help.

# Chapter 14

Another day down and it wasn't getting any easier standing on my feet all day. But I was starting to grasp how to put on a happy face and encourage big tips. With a few hours to burn while I waited for Melody, I carefully transferred the tip money from my work apron to a zipped coin purse. Leaving out just enough money for one cold beer next door, I locked the rest in Melody's car, keeping the temptation of drinking more out of reach. I grappled with buying a pack of smokes, and declined that idea as well. Above the mahogany bar a sign read, "Eat, drink and be merry for tomorrow you might die (or be in Utah)". This, of course, was making fun of Utah's' strict alcohol regulations. A perfunctory smile played on my lips.

Life had brought an unexpected turn of events in my life. Who would have guessed that I would be in Utah, working in a restaurant? Although I still felt much like a prisoner, held against my will, Melody and I had settled into a comfortable acceptance of each other's differences. And it was good to be making real wages.

Nudging off my shoes, and rubbing my sore feet, my mind zip lined to Brad. Now there was someone that couldn't be any different than me. I started mentally reviewing all the differences: he was male (yes, he was!) and I was female; he had a future, I didn't; he was a Christian, I wasn't; he was focused, I lived for the next buzz; he was smart, intelligent, I was an idiot; he was at peace, I was in a state of constant turmoil; he had goals, I lived for the moment. The quote, "Opposites attract" flitted in my head, and I smirked out loud, "Not *that* much opposite!"

"What's that?" The bartender looked over at me quizzically.

"Oh, nothing. Just laughing at a crazy thought in my head."

"Say, aren't you the one in here the other day hanging around with Joey? He was asking about you."

"If Joey is the loser I had mistaken for a man, tell him to pick on someone his own age."

The bartender laughed, and said, "I'll do just that."

The first week melted into two, then three. I was well aware that I had more than enough for a bus fare home, but I found myself putting off the purchase of a ticket. Melody, Carmen and I spent a lot of time doing things I never would have considered fun even a month ago. Even hiking in the immense granite splendor of the Rocky Mountains became enjoyable to me, as my legs had strengthened from my job, and my lungs had begun to clear out the black soot, that used to leave me wheezing. I was struck by the splendor and plethora of wildflowers, some so delicate, and others boasting their bright yellows and oranges. A niggling thought arose in my heart that no one had planted these beauties, yet they had a perfect design and color scheme. On more adventuresome days, we would hike up to hidden lakes and waterfalls, and I began to understand what Melody meant to breathe deep and enjoy the clear air, lacking humidity and bugs.

There were times when conversation with Carmen and Melody would lapse into "God" talk, and I would choose to not participate. But thankfully, neither one of them would force me to participate in their talks, or to voice my own opinion. There were nights when I would lay awake missing my old life, and also sensing that something besides my old life was lacking in my life. I know Melody would say the gaping hole could be filled by God. Whether or not there was a God, I was convinced that if He did exist, He was an old ogre, either unaware of the pain on Earth, or simply didn't care. Melody often described Him as her Father. Only knowing my own dad, I wasn't impressed.

Then one night, my sister Katie called. "Grace, how *are* you? I have thought of you so much since our last phone call. I hated the way it ended. Are you doing alright?"

I'm fine, Katie, how are you doing?"

"Well, I'm feeling terrible about not letting you come home. I've been talking with Shelley. You are a grown woman, and you are our sister. We have pooled together some money, and can buy you a plane ticket to come home. You are welcome to stay with either one of us."

So there it was, the defining moment. This is what I had wanted, right? Then why was I hesitating? "Hey, wow, that sounds great. Katie, I don't think I told you that I have a job now as a waitress working with Melody. She got me the job, so it would only be fair for me to give them two week's notice."

"Grace, that's terrific! Are you starting to like it out there?"

"I didn't say *that*, but I am making money. Maybe I'll just finish out the summer, and head back home in the fall. I hear the winters out here are pretty intense, and Melody rents out her extra rooms in the winter. I do miss you and Shelley, though . . . and friends."

"Well, you sound good. You know we miss you, too, but it sounds like maybe you are making a life out there." Katie gushed on for a few more minutes, with the promise to call again soon.

Humph. A life? That's what you call this? I guess it could be worse. Yes, I knew what worse was.

Most mornings, Brad would be one of the first customers of the day. He would typically weave his way around tables, and invariably sit

in my designated area. At first, I thought it might be a coincidence, but I began to admit he was purposefully sitting where he knew I would wait on him. I was embarrassed to admit that his choice of seating, did make me feel somewhat elated. However, he seemed to avoid me by burying his nose in his books. Besides telling me his order, we didn't have much more we talked about. So it came as a surprise when Brad actually looked up and gave me his charming smile. Melody had informed me that Brad was finishing his degree by the end of summer, and was frantically trying to get all his assignments completed and also work full time on top of that.

"Heard you and your two amigos have been doing some hiking lately. Wish I had more time for things like that, but I have been swamped this summer. I'm not sure if you know, but I work at Coles Sport, a four season sports store. We're having a huge summer sale on hiking boots and clothing. If you are interested, you ought to come check it out."

This was obviously not a come on, but it was the first time he had said that much to me. "I don't have wheels to get around. Maybe I can convince Melody to take me sometime."

"It's only a few blocks from here. If you aren't too tired after you're done with your shift, head down. It's a few blocks down on the right."

It did sound better than waiting in a hot car or hanging out with the bartender across the street. I was nodding yes, when I felt his sea green eyes diving into mine. It was one of those moments. You know what I'm talking about. Something clicks, something strums across your heart strings, and you are left wondering if that same sizzling feeling was reciprocated. Mercifully, someone called out for more coffee, and I scurried away like a scared mouse. *I'm not ready to go there, or name what just happened.* After my shift was over, I sat in the hot car sweating and waited for Melody.

# Chapter 15

Brad's head shot up every time the bell hanging over Coles front door jangled, alerting the staff of a new customer coming in. Brad realized he wasn't a Romeo when it came to females. But he had presumed that when the time came, God would find the girl, smooth the path of dating, which would eventually lead to marriage, and then experience a happily ever after. "With two children, and a white picket fence," he chuckled. He felt confused about Grace. She was definitely pretty, but that wasn't supposed to be the only prerequisite to finding a soul partner. She wasn't a Christian, and she often seemed mad at the world. Grace portrayed herself as a strong woman, but inside he felt she had a soft loving heart, a heart that had been chinked by circumstances, but still there under all her layers.

He reviewed in his mind the conversation he had with Grace that morning. Something definitely sparked when he looked in her eyes. He hoped she hadn't notice the sweat that beaded on his forehead, or the way his heart quickened. He had met a lot of pretty women, some who he had been attracted to, some that were also Christians. He really needed to get alone with God. Graduation was looming nearer, and he had spent most of his free time finalizing projects, skipping the valuable time he typically devoted to God. No wonder he was confused. Didn't the Bible explicitly promise that, "God is not the author of confusion, but of peace?" So the obvious conclusion, Brad realized, is that this is not from God."

# Chapter 16

Because of a DUI I had received in Michigan, I didn't have a valid drives license. That never stopped me from driving back home, but I was fairly certain that Melody would never let me drive without one. Realizing I was paralyzed without a car, I set about finding out what it would take to be able to drive again. After many futile phone call and letters, I decided to take a chance and just go to the DMV and say I needed to get a driver's license. The problem was, I couldn't ask Melody or Carmen, as they both knew my story, and I needed to fudge a little bit on the truth. Brad hadn't been in for breakfast for several days, but there he sat, in the same area, and I was going to ask him. As I approached his table I couldn't help but wonder what aftershave he used. It always reminded me of the scent of pine trees and the clean smell after the rain. It would have been easy to ask a simple favor of any other guy I'd known, but Brad was definitely a different animal. Somehow not being completely honest to this guy wasn't something I was proud of, but I still needed a ride.

"Hey, Brad. What are you in the mood for? Pancakes or eggs this morning?" I plunked down his coffee, and put my hand on my hips. "Where have you been? Everyone's been missing you."

"I've been home trying to save some money by making my own breakfast; meaning, I pour some cereal in a bowl and add milk. And does the 'everyone' include you?"

"Don't forget you were my first customer, and my only real regular customer. Brad, I was wondering if I could ask a really big favor?"

"Well, you sure can ask. What is it?" His green eyes twinkled, and for a moment, I believed he might have missed me too.

"I need a ride to the Department of Motor Vehicles to get my driver's license. Would you happen to have any time to take me?"

"Today I can't, or tomorrow, but Thursday I will have some free time in the afternoon. Can you wait until then?"

"Of course! Thanks a million. I sure do appreciate it. Now, eggs or pancakes?"

"Make it eggs over medium with lots of butter on the toast, and a double side of bacon. And I'll pick you up right here on Thursday at noon. Will that work?"

"Yes, sir, and your breakfast is on me today." I did a little sashaying back to the kitchen, and knew full well that I was being watched.

It was gradually getting easier to wake up each morning. By the time Thursday morning came, I was up and dressed before Melody even needed to knock. I found myself taking extra care with my makeup. The night before I had made sure my uniform was clean and wrinkle free. It seemed like decades ago since I had last taken my driver's test. I hoped that I still could remember most of the answers if I was able to get as far as taking the test. It occurred to me that it would also be required of me to take an actual road test. I wondered if Brad was alright with me using his car. At noon, I realized that the car was actually an old beater Chevy truck. That is Brad. Baseball, Hot Dogs, Apple Pie and Chevrolet. The good all American guy. Who was I kidding hanging out with him? Well, he didn't know the real me, first of all. Second, I wasn't about to let him find out. Third, what did it matter? All he was doing was helping me out. Isn't that what any good Christian man should do?

The smell of Brad permeated the truck, in a definitely good way. I guessed that he had done some cleaning, since there was an absence of any litter or any sign of his books that seemed to be always with him. I figured he must own a black dog, though, because no amount of vacuuming could get all that hair off. "Hope I didn't take you away from anything, Brad. This is really important to me, so thanks."

"It's hard to turn down a pretty girl. Hop in. There's no air conditioning, except the good old 4/60 kind. Four windows down going sixty miles an hour."

I rolled my eyes, and let out a sigh. "Ok, buster, get this old jalopy rolling." If my friends could see me now.

# Chapter 17

There was no way for figuring out why he had said yes to Grace. He had an extensive list of all the things he needed to do on Thursday, and here he was driving to pick Grace up to take her to the DMV. Of course, the DMV was near the top of the list for the five worst places to go. But under the grumbling, he was anticipating spending time with Grace, and trying to peel back some layers to the real person. He debated whether to open the door for her, but she was already hopping in before he could make a decision. Apparently she wasn't expecting him to.

Grace was an enigma. When she didn't think anyone was watching, her body language signaled a life that was rudderless and alone, carrying the burdens of the world. When talking with someone, the mask came on that allowed people to think she was tough, resilient, and in control. Right now, she was wearing that mask, and being a little coy and flirtatious as she described her day. By the time they had reached the DMV, Brad had found out that Grace had a dimple on the left side of her cheek, and that she was less confident of herself than she tried to reveal.

Grace insisted that Brad stay in the truck while she went inside. Knowing that it may take a while, he said he'd rather come in, and dug out some books from behind the seat. At least he might get in some studying. With birth certificate in hand, she stood in line and waited for her name to be called. When asked if she had ever had a driver's license before, she looked over at Brad then confidently said no. Within the hour, she had taken and passed the written test. She fidgeted while she waited for the instructor to give the road test. Brad could have guessed that she would pass this test, too. She was one determined young lady. After another hour, she was smiling down at a picture of herself smiling back to her, holding an official Utah driver's license.

"Amazing," she shook her head with wonder. "What you can do with self confidence."

All the way home she recounted to Brad in amusing antics of how she had nearly put the instructor through the windshield, since she had never driven his truck before. "I was so relieved that the truck wasn't a stick shift, although I do know how to drive a stick. Parallel parking wasn't that easy, either, but I was close enough. I think the instructor just wanted to be done with me."

Brad stopped at a red light and watched a mother and child skipping cross the street. Brad felt Grace tense, and when he glanced over, Grace had paled, and the hard resentful countenance had returned. "Is that someone you know?"

"No, just take me home." Brad dropped her off at Melody's house, and Grace disappeared into the cabin with just a curt thank you. It would be a relief to go home to Maggie, one of the few females in his life that did make sense.

# Chapter 18

Somehow being around Brad and his squeaky cleanness made me feel even dirtier. As I watched the young child reach for her mother's hand as they crossed the street, my throat had tightened, and I had to look away. I know Brad was puzzled by my response. Who wouldn't be? A serene picture of a mother and child shouldn't bring out a violent reaction. Except for people like me. People like me who could flirt a little with men like Brad, but could never be more to him than a close acquaintance.

I found Melody out on the deck reading a book. The intense sun and blue skies still astonished me, and how easily at this high altitude the sun could set your skin ablaze. Melody looked up from her reading with her sprite like smile, "Hey, where have you been? Was that Brad's truck I saw just now pulling away?"

"The answer to your first question is I was getting my driver's license." I pulled out my freshly made Utah driver's license with a grin.

Melody's eyebrows shot up in the universal sign of skepticism. "How did you work that out?"

"I heard somewhere that states aren't always connected by the same system. So, I am official. The answer to your next question is, yes, Brad took me. And he is taking me next week for step two to my freedom."

"Ok, what is step two?" Melody's tone sounded hesitant.

"Don't worry, Mel. I'm not going to ask to borrow your car. I know it would go against your morals to hand over keys to someone with my record. That's why next week Brad has agreed to take me to Salt Lake and buy my own car. That is step two."

"That's a big step, Grace. But hey, I'm not your guardian. And Brad is a great guy to take with you to shop for good deals." Melody looked back down at her book and I felt like I had been dismissed. Why did she always make me feel like I was some criminal?

I glanced over at the tiny ruby-throated hummingbirds, dashing in to grab a drink from the feeder, and then darting away. Melody told me that there was a common folk belief in Mexico that hummingbirds bring love and romance. Of course, that is just a legend, but what is truth is that these tiniest of birds must feed every ten minutes or so all day, and they may consume two thirds of their body weight in a single day, mostly in sugar that they get from flower nectar and tree sap, and people like Melody, who faithfully fill the feeders with sugar water.

Next Thursday at noon, Brad pulled up again in his truck while I waited outside of Mt. Air. This time a hefty black dog, with a pink lolling tongue sat in the middle of the front seat. "Hi Grace. Hope you don't mind Molly coming along with us. I really feel bad leaving her home so much."

As I hopped up into the cab of the truck, Molly swiped me with a big fat dog kiss. "Aaaggh," I wiped off the slobber from my face, and gave her a long look. "So, you like the smell of bacon and eggs, do you?"

Brad gave me a sideway glance, and chortled, "I think it's you she likes!"

Molly's large body kept both Brad and me from sneaking glimpses of each other. Once in awhile, Molly would look over at me, and I would flip up my arm in defense of another wet dousing. I hadn't been to Salt Lake since I had first arrived. It felt good to have the wind in my face, and the thrill of buying my first car ever. Brad drove us to

State Street where there was an assortment of car lots. "What kind of car are you looking for, Grace?"

"A cheap one, I guess. I don't know very much about cars. Maybe you have a suggestion?" It wasn't easy talking through a Lab.

Brad pulled into a used car lot. It seemed within seconds a salesman was greeting us and showing me some incredible deals. After taking a few cars on test drives, I settled for a 1970 Monte Carlo. Brad warned me that it was a rear-wheel-drive, which didn't do well in the snow, and because it was a V8, it wouldn't do well at the gas pumps. But it was a sleek coupe style, black exterior, great sound system, and I was sold.

"I'll take it!" I shouted even as I watched Brad give his head a slight shake. Leaning into the salesman, Brad talked quietly nodding his head, and then watching the salesman shake his head. Fifteen minutes later we had a deal, a much lower price than the one listed on the windshield. Now to see if I qualified for a loan for the remaining balance. Brad took Molly for a walk, as I went to a back room and filled out papers. I left the office an hour later, beaming, with keys in hand.

"It's mine!" Molly ran up to me and nudged me, joining in my enthusiasm.

"Before you head back up the hill, I wanted to ask you if you and Melody wanted to come to an end of the summer party. It's partly to celebrate my graduation, but also for everyone to meet a good friend of mine, who is moving out here to live."

"Oh, when is it?" My mind was only partially connected to what Brad was saying. My heart was thrilled at the thought of having my own car, and being able to come and go whenever I wanted.

"Not this Saturday, but the next. We're going to meet at Deer Creek Reservoir. I have a ski boat reserved, and of course we will grill some burgers and brats. I hope you can come."

Water skiing was something I liked to do. I was pleasantly surprised that Brad had invited me. Of course, he had invited Melody too. Since my calendar wasn't what you would call 'booked", I agreed.

"I'll follow you home, just to make sure that old Monte will make it."

"Actually, can I follow you? I'm not sure how to get back to Melody's. Just keep checking on me in the rearview mirror once in awhile. And, uh, thanks, Brad. Glad you were here to help me."

I hopped exuberantly into my new set of wheels, cranked up the radio to what my father used to refer to nerve wracking decibels, and hit the pedal. Freedom! What enjoyment flying up the canyon, and when I got to the place where I knew my way home, I floored the gas pedal and sped around Brad like he was standing still. I gave him a nasty grin as I passed.

Melody made spaghetti for dinner, and I did the dishes. I was anxious to go into town and not have to spend another night watching *The Bill Cosby Show*. As I walked out the door, Melody glanced up from the TV and said, "Be careful". Sometimes I felt like she thought I was a teenager, and she was my mother. Maybe she was just being nice, but she really could rub me the wrong way.

Finding my way to Park City was easy after all the trips to work each morning. Historic Main Street, Park City was a quaint area filled with restaurants, art galleries, and t-shirt shops. The buildings were old, with stores and restaurants sandwiched together. The town looked magical in the twilight hours. If I cocked my head back far enough, I could still see splotches of snow on the tops of the mountains, even this late in summer. There was a fresh evening coolness in this alpine town. With autumn quickly approaching, I found the crisp evening air invigorating. A midweek night in the summer was not the liveliest place, but there were cars and a few motorcycles parked outside of a place called the Claim Jumper. Music wafted outside from the saloon, and I felt if I closed my eyes I could hear the old tinny piano music from the 1800's, and see weary looking miners coming in for a beer after a long day at the silver mine.

I attracted attention as soon as I entered the bar. Quickly surveying they crowd, I realized that I was one of the few females there. Knowing after a few drinks it wouldn't matter, I scrounged up some courage and casually walked in. With relief I heard someone call my name, and recognized a breakfast customer. Seeing he was alone, I flopped down on a stool next to him and ordered a Pink Lady, knowing full well, that was the first order for that drink that night.

"Hey,Thad," I was impressed I could recall his name. We chatted and gossiped for awhile and then I threw out the million dollar question. "Do you believe in God?"

"Now, Grace, haven't you heard you never discuss religion or politics?"

"I'm not discussing, just asking." I ordered another drink. Tucked in my mind was the promise I had made to myself not to drink more than two drinks. After all I had a new car, and I did have to work in the morning. Was that called, responsibility?

"I'm not in the mood to go deep with this, but let's just say that when I first started studying to be an optometrist, we studied the eye in depth. In spite of what I was taught in school, there is no way that an eye could have evolved. No way."

I returned his gaze with curiosity. "You are an optometrist?"

"Not exactly. I dropped out when I discovered skiing, and just couldn't force myself into four more years of college."

"What do you think of Christians, Thad? I mean, do you think they are for real?"

"My grandmother was a Christian, and one of the sweetest women you could ever meet. She really lived her faith. Then there are those who say they are, and are some of the worst people I know. I don't know, Grace. That's a tough question. But right now, I need to scoot home. I have to work in the morning."

"Where do you work now that you aren't going to school anymore?"

"I work at the ski resort in the winter, but right now I am working part time at Cole Sports."

"Ah, do you know Brad Halverson?"

"Sure do. Great guy. You ought to get home yourself, Grace. The breakfast crowd starts pretty early. G'night."

He was right. It was time to go home. The stars were out when I headed for my car. How clear and radiant they looked. Twinkling like diamonds, just like the song. My tires crunched over the gravel stones in Melody's driveway, magnified by the quietness of the night. In the stillness a neighbor's dog barked. The lights in Melody's bedroom were on. I softly whispered, "I'm home."

"See you in the morning, Grace. Good night."

It felt good to crawl under the covers. Maybe it was the drinks or just the beauty of the night, but I felt a Presence with me. I smiled as I buried my head in the cool crisp sheets and fell asleep.

# Chapter 19

Brad was under pressure to finish assignments and take finals before graduation on Friday. He shook his head in wonder why he had given up the last two free Thursdays afternoons to help Grace. He looked down at the only girl in his life right now, Molly, who was bemoaning the lack of exercise and attention. It was funny how Molly had taken an instant partiality to Grace. They say dogs have an inherent talent of being able to recognize kindhearted people. Right now though, Friday couldn't come soon enough. Randy was flying in Friday night, and then he was looking forward to spending time catching up with his friend, and spending a celebrative day at the lake. He silently thanked God for bringing him this far. From a rebellious teenager, to a responsible adult, with little to no support from his family. He knew that all that was because of knowing he was loved unconditionally by a loving Father, more than he could ever imagine. He thought of a pair of sapphire blue eyes, and wanted her to know that she was loved so very much, too. He knew somewhere along the way, life had stung her. He felt a strong urge to mend her shattered heart, and put the pieces back together. He thought of the verse in Isaiah 61 that Jesus was sent to heal the brokenhearted . . . to comfort all who mourn . . . to give them beauty for ashes, the oil of joy for mourning, the garment of praise for the spirit of heaviness. That they may be called trees of righteousness, the planting of the Lord, that God may be glorified. A sweet small Voice whispered in his heart, "*Pray for her, Brad. She is my child.*"

# Chapter 20

Saturday morning's western sky was painted with shades of pink, yellow and red, a sure promise of a spectacular day ahead. I woke up before Melody, which was a rarity. Soon after measuring out two scoops, the aroma of strong black fresh brewed coffee filled the kitchen. Mel and I were in charge of bringing potato salad as our contribution to the picnic. While I waited for the water to boil for the potatoes, I took a hearty mug of coffee and padded out to the deck. The bird feeders had attracted grosbeaks, chickadees, and other species of birds that warbled and twittered gaily in the morning sunshine. I watched with humor, wondering what made them so happy, without fear or concern of what life might bring. The big noisy magpies made a ruckus, chattering loudly to a possible mate. Donning a red robe that was alluring for the hummingbirds, I chuckled at the thought of me looking like a giant feeder to them.

Yesterday after work, I went shopping for a bathing suit. The one I brought from home wasn't what I would feel comfortable in with this group of do-gooders. As I sipped from my coffee cup, I realized I was really excited to have a day out.

A sleepy Melody accompanied me on the deck, cupping a steaming mug of coffee in her hands. We watched in comfortable silence, all the airborne feathered friends. After a few minutes, I went inside to check on the potatoes, and came out with the coffee pot. Refilling both of our cups I said, "You know, this is quite an unreal arrangement we have. You being such a good person with me a, well . . . bad person."

"Wait a minute, Grace. What in the world ever gave you the idea that I am a good person? I am far from good! The Bible says that no one is good except One, and He died on a cross two thousand years ago."

"Oh, you know what I mean. Someone that follows the Ten Commandments, and does that kind of stuff."

"In God's book, 'good' means being without sin. I am definitely not that. I have sinned, do sin, and will sin. Please don't think of me higher that I deserve. If I was without sin, I wouldn't need a Savior. I wouldn't need to be forgiven. But we all need that, Grace."

"But I know everyone thinks that you are a better person than I am. I don't think you know all that I have done."

"Nor do I want to know. I'm trying to think how you might understand how I believe, and what the Bible says. Let's use your words in describing two people who are trying to jump to the peak of that mountain." Melody pointed to a distant mountain on the right. "Let's say there is a 'good' athlete that has trained and prepared, eaten healthy, followed all the rules and regulations of becoming a super toned fit specimen. He stands on this deck and makes a running leap, trying with all his might to make it to the peak of the mountain. How far does he go? Can he make it to the mountain peak by being in good form? No way. Now let's try someone that is in 'bad' shape. He hasn't trained; he has broken all the rules in getting fit. He makes a flying leap, and he too, falls pitifully short. The moral of the story? Being 'good' doesn't cut it. If the mountain is God's holiness, we all fall short."

Scrunching up my face I floundered, "So if that is true, a murderer and a Nobel peace prize winner are in the same boat. I'm not buying that."

"Some of the greatest heroes in the Bible, Paul, David, Moses were also murderers. Grace, without God's forgiveness we are all without hope."

"So let's say someone was sleeping with all kinds of men, doing drugs, maybe even helped participate in a murder. Are you saying this same person can just say I'm sorry and everything is just dandy? Nice, try."

"Have you heard of the story about the woman at the well?"

"No, and if this is a Bible story, I'd rather not hear it.

"Come on," Melody pleaded, "just listen. I'll try to tell it quickly. Jesus was traveling through Samaria, a place that was really looked down on by the Jews. He was tired and his disciples, those that followed Jesus and were being taught by Jesus, had gone to town to get some food. So Jesus sat by the well around noon, which was the hottest part of the day, and not necessarily when the women of the town would come draw water. But a woman did come, and Jesus asked her for a drink of water. There were two reasons why this was strange. First, as I said, Jews did not associate with Samaritans, but second Jesus was talking to a woman. In those days, and still today in parts of the Middle East, women were second class citizens. So she was surprised and asked Him why He was asking her for a drink. He answered, "If you knew the gift of God and who it is that asks you for a drink, you would have asked Him and He would have given you living water." So she asks where she can get this living water. And He answers "Everyone who drinks this water will be thirsty again, but whoever drinks the water I give them will never thirst." So of course, the woman wants this water, so she won't get thirsty again and have to keep coming to the well. Then this is the neat part. He says to go call your husband and come back. She replies that she has no husband. Jesus said to her, "You are right when you say you have no husband. The fact is, you have had five husbands, and the man you now have is not your husband. What you have just said is true." The woman wonders if He is the Messiah because He knows all about her, and He says that yes, it is HE."

"Okay, nice story. Then I suppose she tells all her friends, and they all believe."

"Actually, that is what happened."

"And what does this all have to do with me?" I shifted in my seat.

"Because we are all the woman at the well . . . longing to taste freedom, to taste the living water. Jesus is that living water. Some refuse to drink, and they remain in chains, ever thirsty. But some realize the truth about themselves, and know that if they but drink that living water they will be forever changed."

I knew I should respond with some sarcastic reply, but nothing seemed to come to me. I drained my coffee cup, and stood up. "Well, guess we better get making that potato salad.

The tension that hung heavy earlier dissipated as we cried over the chopped onions, and laughed at our differing opinions of how much mustard to use. After gathering up towels, coolers and suntan lotion we headed out. I offered to drive, as Melody hadn't been acquainted with old Monte yet. Rolling down the windows and cranking up the radio to an Eagles song, Melody and I sang our hearts out, and it felt good.

People were already out boating when we got there, but I glimpsed Brad and another guy throwing ice into a cooler. Most of the group I didn't know, but was glad when Brad and his buddy sauntered over and introduced us.

"Melody, Grace, this is my friend Randy. He got in last night, and still is getting used to being in Utah." Randy was a stocky, muscular fireplug, with lots of energy and a kind smile. He nodded at both of us, but seem to linger a second longer at Melody.

"You ready to ski, Grace?" Glancing over at Brad, I was struck anew at his strong jaw, proud straight nose, and kind eyes that matched the color of the water.

We walked over to the boat, as two girls disembarked. Although wet and shivering, they congratulated Brad on his graduation and introduced themselves to me as Carol Ann and Julie.

"Oh, Brad! I forgot to congratulate you. How did it all go?" I felt dense forgetting why we were even there. Carol Ann and Julie gave us a wave, as we jumped in and took off with a roar. I was the first one to get in to the chilly water. An artery to my past was reconnected when I shouted "Hit it!" and felt the exhilaration of the boat lifting me out of the water onto the glassy water's surface. Feeling the waters spray as I left the safe area behind the boat to lean to the left, jump the wake, and hurl myself as far out as possible, made me giddy. Watching all the smiles and thumbs up from the boat, I felt a sense of reckless happiness, a feeling that had been alien to my life for some time. The four of us in the boat took several turns each before heading back to shore. Randy switched places with me. Snapping my towel out on the sand, I plopped down and let the diminishing heat of the sun, kiss my upturned face.

It couldn't have been more than a few minutes when a shadow blocked the sun. Squinting upward, a tall hippie looking guy, bare chest with well worn bell bottom pants, smiled down at me. "Can I sit down?"

"Can't stop ya," I mumbled.

Sitting cross legged, he tucked some strands of hair behind his ear. "I'm Jake. You looking for some fun?"

"What kind of fun?" I ventured

"I'm talking about flying high tonight. You understand?"

"Why are you asking me? Why pick me? Why not anyone else sitting on the beach? Why me?" My voice grew steadily higher.

"Hey, man, chill out. Just thought you looked like you might want to party right tonight."

"I'm not a man, by the way. Tell me, do I look different from the rest of the group?"

"You just look like you like to have fun. Those people look like boring, man. Am I wrong? Come on. I got some fun candy back at the camper we're staying in."

Apparently sensing my hesitation, Jake formed a slow moving smile, and smirked, "I thought I knew a party girl when I saw one."

Just then Carmen called over. "Grace, can you help us gather some firewood? We are about to start the grill and light the campfire."

I looked over at Jake and winked, "Looks like you thought wrong."

"Whatever, sister. You have a real fine time with those folks." He stood up and wiped off his backside from sand, and meandered off.

I sat there for a few more minutes, watching the fading sun start sinking into the water. I watched the water lap onto the shore, and looked up at the cloudless sky. I nodded, stood up, and helped find firewood.

Why is it that the combination of water and sun can leave you ravenous? After changing into dry clothes in the restroom, I dug out our potato salad and added it to the tempting array of other dishes lined up on the picnic table. Looking for Melody, I found her talking to Randy and a few guys I had never seen before. Feeling a little out of place, I looked around for something to do.

"Are you as good at horseshoes as you are at skiing?" Brad grinned at me and motioned me over to the horseshoe pit. It was a relief to hear someone yell later that the food was ready, as I was getting whipped pretty soundly at throwing horseshoes. Piling my plate high, I found a log to sit on, and balanced my food on my knee.

"Want anything to drink? Brad was digging though the ice chest.

"You have any beer?"

"It's actually not allowed on a public beach," Brad replied. "Can I get you anything else?"

I smiled to myself thinking any other party I had been to wouldn't have stopped us from bringing alcohol, legal or not. Spying a can near the top I answered, "Alright, how about the next best thing? I'll have a Dad's Root Beer."

Melody sat down next to me. Before I knew it the air began getting a faint chill, as the sun started dropping in the west. Scrunching up my nose, I could feel that I had gotten some sun today. As darkness started to fall, a guy named Pete took out his guitar. Soon I heard myself joining in with the rest of the group singing some silly campfire songs. With the campfire crackling and the stars starting to poke out, I felt a delicious sense of contentment. Somewhere along the way, the music transitioned to songs about Jesus, and there was a hushed reverence in their singing. Not knowing the words, I began to feel out of place again, and the words of Jake's earlier comment came back to haunt me. Glancing over at Melody, I saw that she had closed her eyes. She had her hands and face raised to the sky. By the glow of the campfire, I saw a radiance I knew that I didn't have. Jake was right.

I stood up and went in search of my beach bag. Brad materialized out of the darkness. "Where are you headed?"

"Guess it's time to head home."

"So soon? Didn't Melody ride with you?"

Peering over at the group circled around the campfire, I smirked. "Those are her friends. Someone will give her a ride home." I gave him a smug smile and headed to my car.

Melody didn't seem all that happy to see me in the morning. I had heard her come home later that night, but she hadn't stopped at my bedroom door to let me know she was home. I set out a bowl of cereal and a glass of juice for her. I could tell she was dressed and ready for church. Good. I could have some time alone. After hearing her car's tires crunching on the gravel as she pulled out of the driveway. I changed my pajamas for some hiking clothes. Filling a canteen with water, I headed out the back door, where a trail was easily accessible.

Initially I needed to choose to go right or left. Going right would cover fairly flat terrain. Left would lead me to a steep vertical incline but a fantastic view at the end. I chose to go left, thinking a good sweat would be good for me. After climbing for nearly an hour on a trail that was a mere trace through towering trees, I sat down on a slab of rock. From this position I could look down on Park City. Taking a big swig of water, I closed my eyes and listened to the sound of the wind rustling the leaves. It was hard to believe that some of the leaves at this elevation were already starting to turn. Fall wasn't too far off. Winters came early here. What were my plans? I had told Melody when I first arrived that I wouldn't stay long. Here it was approaching fall, and I had no clue what to do. It was evident that Melody needed to rent out my room this winter. As I thought of my life back home, I had to admit that I wasn't nearly as anxious to get back home as when I first arrived. Maybe I wasn't the same person that had left several months ago. Thinking of the party last night, I knew I didn't belong with that crowd either. I was in a sort of a limbo not belonging to either world. I was determined not to always be this in-between person. I watched as my shadow moved ahead of me as we walked together, the little girl of the past and the woman I wanted to be.

A blue jay hopped next to me and cocked his head as if he were pondering my life dilemma with me. Why did life have to be so confusing? Taking another swig of water, I continued back down the trail. Hearing a rustling to my left, I watched a doe leap out from behind some bushes and bound away. *I won't hurt you*, I whispered. She stopped and turned her graceful head and watched me out of large brown eyes. *It's a scary world, pretty lady, but I won't hurt you.* By the time I got home, I saw Melody's car in the driveway.

Melody was in the kitchen whipping up something in a bowl. "Hey, Mel, how was church?" I was hoping to keep my voice sounding upbeat.

"Oh, hi, Grace. It was good. Listen; there are some friends from last night coming over for lunch in a few minutes. I think you know most of them."

Startled I made a polite cough, and told her I was planning on heading into town anyway.

"Oh, please don't. I need you to help me make a salad. I have chicken in the oven and I'm making banana bread."

"Mel, I'll help you make a salad, but I'm not planning on hanging out with your friends."

"What's wrong with you, Grace? What happened last night that you would leave me without a ride?"

"Oh, I knew you would find a ride with one of *your* friends."

"What's eating you? They are your friends too. Sometimes I just don't understand you."

"Well, that makes two of us. I don't understand you, either."

Melody exhaled with a loud sigh "What is happening in town that you can't stay?"

"Okay, I'll tell you. I don't feel comfortable with your friends. It's not that they aren't nice, it's just that they aren't who I would pick out as my own friends."

Melody eyed me with frustration. “It’s not like you have to spend the rest of your life with them on a deserted island. Alright, if you can just help me here a minute, I’ll try to understand.”

But naturally, while I was making the salad, Carol Ann and Carmen showed up. Then within minutes other cars arrived, and I was stuck. I slunk into my bedroom and changed out of my hiking clothes into a clean pair of shorts and a tee shirt. I could hear Brad and Randy’s voice in the kitchen and then I heard my name mentioned. Wondering how long I could hide out, there came a rapping of knuckles on the door. Apparently not long.

Crossing the room, I hesitantly opened the door. There stood Brad. Since I typically saw him sitting in a booth early in the morning, seeing him standing there tall, leaning against the door frame and looking very manly, seemed a bit surreal.

“We’re about ready to eat. Are you coming?” Brad grinned down at me.

“Sure, in a minute. I have a few things I need to do.” What those things were I wasn’t sure, but I closed the door and sat on the bed and wondered how I got into such messes.

When I came out, Pete was praying and thanking God for the food, and for Melody and Grace being such great hostesses. As if I had a choice.

Melody was giving me a sly grin, and I felt like throwing my lemonade at her. Filling my plate, I headed outside to sit on the deck. A few minutes later others piled out the door, carrying out their plates, laughing and acting like life was a bowl of cherries. It struck me as odd that alcohol or drugs weren’t in their equation of having a good time. Maybe that was what was wrong with me, why these people irritated me. I had spent much of my adult life intoxicated and here I was trying to be a barrel of fun on lemonade with a bunch of church goers. I wonder if any of these people had ever experienced real fun.

Giving a quick glance over to where Brad was talking to Carmen, our eyes met and held, and I frantically turned away, but not before my heart played staccato on my mind.

# Chapter 21

During the course of catching up, Randy admitted to Brad that he had drifted seriously away from God. While enthused about his budding career working for a newspaper, he had fallen fast and hard for a girl in the adjacent cubicle. At first Lisa seemed interested when he talked about his faith. She even came to church a few times with him. But gradually she became less interested, until finally she told him that it was alright to be a little religious, but not to be fanatical about it. So in his desire to please her, he put God on the back burner of his heart. Church took up too much precious time from idyllic Sundays together. After nearly a year of dating, Randy decided to pop the question. On his way over to Lisa's house, he rehearsed a memorable way to ask her to marry him, while Lisa at the same time, was home rehearsing how to tell him that she had reunited with an old college boyfriend.

"It was the hardest time of my life, Brad. I really had thought she was the one. Then it all became so clear that I had foolishly given up the one thing that meant more to me than a career or girlfriend. I was so ashamed. But as you know, the One I had turned my back on, was waiting patiently with love to welcome me back. I heard about a job opening in Salt Lake, and here I am.

The two buddies got ready for church Sunday morning. Brad had wrestled most of the night until his sheets and blankets wound up in a big ball at the end of his bed. Brad's mind whirled as he kept hearing Randy's pain in getting involved with someone that didn't believe like he did. His mind would betray him by moving in his thoughts and resting on a lovely face with pained blue eyes. Why would his thoughts even go there? She was trouble. She rarely smiled, and always seemed so negative. What is attractive in that? He paraded through his mind all the girls he knew. There was a fun, athletic girl he worked with that didn't hide the fact that she was interested in him. Then of course, there were the girls in his church group. He considered Carol Ann, Carmen, Julie, and Melody. All great girls for sure, but there was no spark. Maybe spark came later. He had heard in looking for a mate, you should consider a triangle with three needed sides. First, is she a believer, second, do your personalities click, and third is there an attraction? Often he had met girls that contained two out of the three. Considering Grace, none of them were present. Well, to be honest, maybe there was some attraction. Probably the best advice I could give myself, he thought, is to run.

With that in mind, when he arrived at church, he was disloyal to his own resolve, and found himself searching out Melody to see if by any chance her cousin was with her. Trying to not nurture his disappointment he listened to the pastor give a message of God's Grace. Yep, that was the title.

After church Melody wove her way through the church crowd to ask Brad and Randy over for lunch at her house. Randy accepted quickly, while Brad gave a brief nod, and blustered, "Sure, why not?"

When Brad knocked on Grace's bedroom door that afternoon, he wasn't prepared at what the impact of seeing Grace did to his heart. When he thought of the three sides of the triangle needed for a mate, he knew without a doubt, the attraction side was definitely there.

# Chapter 22

Have you ever woke from a sound sleep, not knowing what it was that caused you to wake with heart hammering, a disturbing feeling of perhaps a dream that you couldn't recall? That happened to me quite frequently. I sat up in bed this particular night, and listened to the night sounds, waiting for my heart to quit drumming. The Three Dog Night song, *One,* claiming that one is the loneliest number that you'll ever do, kept cycling in my mind. I was alone. My sisters called faithfully once a week and I knew they loved me. But out here, there was really no one I felt close to, that I could talk to, share my feelings, my thoughts, and my fears. Shuffling over to the window, I gazed up at a nearly full silent moon shining down on this quiet log cabin, and a woman who hungered to belong.

With anxiety still wrapping itself around my soul, I felt my way into the kitchen. The silence and the darkness dispelled as I snapped on the kitchen light. Filling the tea kettle, and setting it on the stove, I rummaged around for some Chamomile tea. A light in the hall flipped on, and Melody emerged in her pink and yellow pajamas, rubbing her eyes still half immersed in sleep.

"What are you doing up, Grace?" She asked, sweeping a hand over her mouth to cover a yawn.

"Just couldn't sleep. Sorry if I woke you. Want some tea?"

Melody nodded, as she slipped into the chair next to me. "Make sure it doesn't have caffeine in it. We have to work in the morning." She laid a gentle hand over mine. "What's going on, Gracie? You just always seem so sad, sometimes angry."

Horrified, I felt warm tears coursing down my face. Swiping them away angrily, I leaped to get the shrilling tea pot. Pouring the hot water into two mismatched cups, I dipped the tea bags in to let them steep.

"I really want to be your friend, Grace. I really do. I know you feel out of place here, away from your family and friends. I was hoping that you could see me as family and that you could embrace my friends as yours."

"I'm not good enough for your friends, and I know they look down at me. You probably go to church and pray for your sinful cousin."

"Have I or any of my friends ever treated you like that? I don't believe it for a minute. Everyone has a past. Everyone has things we have regretted doing or saying."

I squeezed my eyes shut. "Mel, I tried to have an abortion when I was a teenager. I couldn't go through with it, but the doctor, if I can call him that, had gone far enough that the fetus and my body was so severely infected that the baby died, and I nearly did, too. I wanted to die, and I often wonder why I didn't."

"Sweet Gracie, what a storm you have been through, and I don't think you are seeing calm waters yet. I know you don't want me to preach to you, either. But there is such healing and forgiveness in Jesus. The Bible says that there is now no condemnation for those who are in Christ Jesus. It's as simple as recognizing your need for Him, accepting Him as your Savior. Believing that He died for you. Isn't that what you want? Someone that loves you unconditionally? That has the power to forgive and make you free and clean in Him?"

I dunked my tea bag several times, and contemplated how to answer my cousin. Here we were, sitting in the middle of the night, somewhere in the mountains of Utah, talking about deep soul searching matters. "Mel, you are a friend. And I appreciate your concern for me. But when you say it is simply recognizing my need for Him, well, that's just it. It's too simple. You make it sound like all I have to do is say yes, and life will be perfectly fine."

No, that's not . . ."

"Melody", I interrupted, "I really do appreciate what you're saying. Tonight isn't the time to ponder deep discussions. Drink up your tea, and let's head back to bed. It'll be time to get ready for work before you know it."

My birthday was at the beginning of October. Probably one of the reasons I have always loved the fall season best. I had a feeling that my sisters had called and informed Melody of this less than anticipated event. Every year was a reminder that I was getting older, with absolutely no plans or goals, or for that matter, no purpose. I had taken on the lunch shift with Melody, so we often rode together to save gas. There were times when I had to dig up every ounce of energy to go to work, but other days, there was a sense of security in knowing what I was doing, seeing familiar faces, enjoying light bantering between co-workers, and seeing Brad most mornings.

I heard the phone ringing in the kitchen, and a few minutes later Melody called out that somebody was on the phone for me. Surprised, I switched off *Starsky and Hutch*, and made my way to the phone. "Hello?"

"Hi Grace, its Brad."

A jolt of electricity shot through my body. With what I hoped sounded like nonchalance, I gulped, "Oh hey, Brad. What's up?"

"I heard through the grapevine that it is someone's birthday. Would it be okay if I stopped by later? I have something for you."

"Uh, I guess. You don't have to bring me anything, though. I'm not too excited about adding another year."

When the doorbell eventually rang I hated that my heart was fluttering, and that I had to give a quick look in the hall mirror before I answered the door. And there he was. Confidence sure looked good on him—wish I could wear it like he does. Blue denim shirt, blue jeans, tennis shoes, and a smile that could slay a giant—a female giant anyway.

"Well, come in." With all the rehearsing of what I would say when I saw him, that is what ended up coming out my mouth. His hair looked freshly washed, and his smile was impossible not to respond to.

He produced from behind his back a neatly wrapped pink present with a brown and pink bow.

"Ok, what is it?" I shook the box, felt around, and proclaimed it must be a box of chocolates.

Brad smiled, THAT smile, and told me to open it, and see.

I tore off the bow and ripped it open to find a box with a leather bound Bible inside.

"So, would you be mad if I said I think I would rather have a box of chocolates?" I noticed that my name had been engraved on the front of the Bible. And how did I feel? That was another mystery. It's not that I really wanted a Bible, but it was the fact that someone had cared enough to buy me one. This was something I decided to file away and re-examine at a later time.

"Can I take you for a birthday dinner?" Brad gave me a wry grin.

"Depends on where you are taking me, sir."

"You are going to have to just trust me on this one. Oh, and grab a jacket."

I grabbed a jean jacket from the closet, and shouted down the hall to Melody that I was going out. As we headed out the door, I was surprised to see Molly in the truck, never taking her eyes off the door that had swallowed up her master minutes before. Anticipating the customary dog kiss, I turned my face as I hopped up into Brad's truck. "How ya doing, girl?" I patted her head, and ducked just in time to miss another attempt at my face.

It had been another perfect day. Crisp cool evenings and days that dazzled with the golden aspen leaves dancing in the sun. We were headed into town, and I tried getting a glimpse of Brad to get an idea where we might be going. He pulled into the city park, drove up to an open air wooden pavilion. The park was next to the old Miner's Hospital that had been converted into the local public library several years earlier. I opened the truck door, and 85 pounds of black blur bounded off my lap to the ground. "Aaahh!" I slumped out of the truck and sighed. "What are you laughing at?"

"Just at my crude gallantry. I guess this might be one of the least proper dinner experiences you've ever had."

If you only knew, I thought. That's when I saw Brad dig out a picnic basket, a blanket, and a partially chewed toy for Molly.

"What's this? A picnic?" I was actually thrilled with the idea. Brad spread the blanket on the ground, which Molly immediately claimed as her own. From there we could see kids playing soccer, others playing volleyball, and dogs and owners enjoying a good romp in the cool grass. Deep pink and orange slashes of clouds dispersed over the mountains, smudging the sky like spilled water paints. Opening the wicker basket, we pulled out sandwich meat, cheese, and all the condiments to make a delectable deli sandwich. Added to that was coleslaw, grapes, potato chips, and chocolate chip cookies, complete with plastic forks, plates, napkins. "These cookies look almost homemade." I was arranging the food neatly, and as far away from Molly as I could.

"I've been a bachelor for quite awhile. There are some things I can make quite well." As I crushed some chips to add to my sandwich, I saw Brad stare at me with interest.

"Just a quirky thing I do. I like the crunch of potato chips in my sandwich. You look like I just robbed a bank or something."

That's when I noticed that he had opened his sandwich to layer it with crushed potato chips. Molly cocked her head as we laughed as if to question the sanity of the human race. It was a memorable night. Brad talked about his job he had landed shortly after graduation. Park City was starting to grow, and with growth came a need for architects. He liked the people he worked with and was making fairly good wages. We took turns throwing Molly's toy, and by the time we headed home, she had fallen sound asleep on my lap. When we arrived at Melody's, Brad came around to my side of the truck, and rescued me from a sleepy dog. As he helped me down, I inhaled the masculine scent of him and felt and absorbed his warmth through the layer of his jacket.

"Well, good night. Thanks for a wonderful birthday. Probably the best in a long time." I smiled at him and turned to go.

"I'll walk you to the door." Well, this was almost like a real proper date. We got almost to the door before he stopped me, and said "Wait. Maybe you better brush some of that dog hair off of you."

"Um, I'm fine. Good night."

I pushed open the front door, and a blast of 'Happy Birthdays' greeted me. The living room light exploded with bright happy faces, all looking at me expectantly. I turned around, and Brad greeted me with a broad toothy smile.

"Happy birthday, Grace."

And then I did it again. Tears streamed down my face. The whole party was so unexpected. It really *was* a surprise party.

Melody was lighting candles, while Pete turned out the lights. It was quite the moment in time, when all these people, who felt like aliens to me not too long ago, were singing to me with a warmth that made a cool October night glow with unforgettable memories.

# Chapter 23

Pulling into his driveway, Brad looked over at Randy's new car, and was surprised to see him still sitting in it. Randy was commuting each day to work from Park City to Salt Lake. Brad's little place was snug with the two of them living there, but it had been a blessing to him to have his friend there, to share thoughts and encourage each other in their walk with the Lord. Shutting off the car he glanced up and found the Big and Little Dipper which seemed unusually bright on this clear October night. Shrugging on his jacket, he detected the vapor from his breath with each exhale.

"What are you doing sitting in the car, Rand?"

"Just thought I would say a prayer before you got home. I know this might not be any of my business, but what's with you and Grace, Brad?" Randy climbed out of the car and shoved the door shut.

"What are you talking about?"

"Come on, Bud. It was nice of you to keep Grace away while the party was set up tonight, but I think it's obvious that more is going on here."

"You're right about one thing. It's none of your business."

"Brad, maybe you didn't hear me telling you the story about Lisa, and the mistake I made, the pain that followed. Grace isn't a Christian. You really shouldn't be playing with fire."

Brad twisted his head to meet Randy face to face. "Grace needs a friend. Somebody she can count on."

"That might be true. But maybe that friend should be a female. I saw the way she looked at you tonight, and I saw the way you looked at her, too, bro. I'm just saying to be careful. Let me have made the mistake, and then we both can learn from it."

"She's just so vulnerable and needy, Rand."

"Yes, I see that. The very reason that you can't be her rescuer; you can't be her savior. Right? Huh, buddy? Am I right?" Randy threw his arm around him as they walked to the house.

"So, I have a question for you, Randy." Brad threw down his keys on the kitchen table while Randy turned on some lights. "What's going on with you and Melody?"

"Now that is a good question. Let's just say I am looking into that option."

# Chapter 24

The next week, Brad only came in for breakfast one time. I watched him make his way to a table that wasn't in my section. Granted, my section was nearly full, but it did seem strange. He gave me a curt nod and started reading the paper. Analyzing his every action was childish and immature, and I refused to do it. By the second week, I didn't need to guess anymore. Perhaps Melody had warned him off after I had spilled out one of many dark secrets to her. Who was I kidding anyway? Did I really think there could ever be any future with that guy? Making my way over to where an admirer of mine sat, I winked at him, and said, "I think I'm ready for that movie you've been asking me to."

Which of course was a mistake. It was too bad that the movie wasn't more captivating, which might have kept Hank's mind on the movie and not on me. Declining going for a drink afterword, I purposely stared at my watch, exclaiming how late it was getting. There is a good reason why people become pessimists. Anytime in my life when things ever started looking up, I'd get slammed right back in the pit.

Dawn streamed through the blinds in little rectangular patterns, warning me it was time to get up. Life just seems too hard to face sometimes, and I tugged the covers back over my face, deciding not to go to work. Realizing that not going would leave the staff shorthanded, I was reluctant to tell Melody. When I heard her light knock, I called out, "I'm not feeling well, Mel. I'm staying home."

With concern on her face, she creaked open the door and poked her head inside. "What is it Grace? Stomach ache? Sore throat? What can I get you?"

"Oh, just feeling out of sorts. Sorry to do this to you, and everyone. It makes for a lot more work."

"You just get better. We will be fine. I'll miss you though today . . . and will be praying for you."

I gave a little wave, and crawled back under the covers, and went back to sleep. Somewhere around eleven, I woke up, opened the blinds, and shuffled out to the kitchen to pour some cereal and milk into a bowl. It felt peculiar to be home alone. I pictured the busy transition period at work from breakfast to lunch, and the added work load when someone wasn't there. A little wave of guilt swept over me, along with wondering if a certain customer had shown up this morning. Crossing back into my bedroom, I noticed my birthday present from Brad. The Bible was still tucked neatly in the box. Yanking it out from the box, I carried it over to the bed. Propping up my pillows behind me, I cracked open the Bible, noticing again my name engraved on the cover. The smell of leather and new book aroma drifted from the crisp white pages, and I scrunched into a cozy position, and turned to the first page. This was the first time I had even looked at my present since my birthday over two weeks ago. In Brad's neat writing, he had filled in the blanks with:

*To Grace Norman*

*From your good friend, Brad Halverson*

*May you find peace within these pages, and answers to all your questions.*

I looked out the window. The furnace had come on earlier pushing out stale air from months of summer dormancy. Smoke was rising from the chimney of the neighbor's house, in small arcs and puffs. Glancing down, I flipped several pages. Endless introductions and explanations filled the first dozen pages. I flipped to somewhere in the middle and started reading.

*Psalm 86: A Prayer of David.*

*Hear me, LORD, and answer me,*
*for I am poor and needy.*
*Guard my life, for I am faithful to you;*
*save your servant who trusts in you.*
*You are my God; have mercy on me, Lord,*
*for I call to you all day long.*
*Bring joy to your servant, Lord,*
*for I put my trust in you.*
*You, Lord, are forgiving and good,*
*abounding in love to all who call to you.*
*Hear my prayer, LORD;*
*listen to my cry for mercy.*
*When I am in distress, I call to you,*
*because you answer me.*

*Among the gods there is none like you, Lord;*
*no deeds can compare with yours.*
*All the nations you have made*
*will come and worship before you, Lord;*
*they will bring glory to your name.*
*For you are great and do marvelous deeds;*
*you alone are God.*

*Teach me your way, LORD,*
*that I may rely on your faithfulness;*
*give me an undivided heart,*
*that I may fear your name.*
*I will praise you, Lord my God, with all my heart;*
*I will glorify your name forever.*
*For great is your love toward me;*
*you have delivered me from the depths,*
*from the realm of the dead.*

*Arrogant foes are attacking me, O God;*
*ruthless people are trying to kill me—*
*they have no regard for you.*
*But you, Lord, are a compassionate and gracious God,*
*slow to anger, abounding in love and faithfulness.*
*Turn to me and have mercy on me;*
*show your strength in behalf of your servant;*
*save me, because I serve you*
*just as my mother did.*
*Give me a sign of your goodness,*
*that my enemies may see it and be put to shame,*
*for you, LORD, have helped me and comforted me.*

My eyes shifted back to the top. *A Prayer of David.* Was that the David that Melody told me had murdered someone? Skimming through the verses again I read, *When I am in distress, I call to you, because you answer me.* Further down, I read, *But you, Lord, are a compassionate and gracious God slow to anger, abounding in love and faithfulness.*

*Turn to me and have mercy on me; show your strength in behalf of your servant;*

*save me, because I serve you just as my mother did. Give me a sign of your goodness . . .*

My eyes drifted back to the window, then down at my hands. They were trembling, touching the words I had just read.

# Chapter 25

Brad roused himself early enough to take Molly for a walk, giving himself enough time to shower, shave and get ready for work. The late October morning left frost on the ground, and a clear crisp chill in the air, with light fog settling wraith like in low lying areas. Molly lived for mornings like this. She barked and danced in pure bliss, as Brad heaved her toy countless times, chuckling at Molly's intense desire to retrieve, mindless of smells, dogs, or trekkers walking by.

Brad admitted to himself, that breakfasts hadn't been the same lately. Grabbing a banana, or a quick bowl of cereal, didn't have the same appeal as being waited on and delivered savory hot food. Randy left early for his commute to Salk Lake, leaving a quiet house. So chatting with acquaintances while sharing a cup of coffee had its advantages, and watching a certain waitress's slow grin spread over her flushed face when she saw him come in, did too. Brad pondered again why he had spent the last few weeks avoiding her. What Randy said made a lot of sense, and yet he felt there was a reason why Grace had come into his life. Maybe God was using him to reach into her soul in a way others couldn't.

# Chapter 26

Three plates were waiting under the warming shelf to be delivered to a hungry breakfast crowd. I deftly lined them up my arm, and began making my way to the designated table. From the corner of my eye, I saw Brad walk in. With a smile, I called out, "Nice to see you again, stranger."

Brad tipped his hat, and worked his way to an open table in my section. It was several minutes before I brought the coffee pot over and took his order. "We started thinking that you were patronizing more upscale restaurants in the area."

He shook his head in amusement. "Not in a million."

Brad seemed to be a in a good mood which put me in a good mood and even more so when he asked me what I was doing that night.

"Probably doing some laundry or something else as exciting. Why do you ask?"

He seemed to gather his thoughts. "Molly was wondering if you might want to take a hike around Deer Valley. She is pretty partial to some ponds there, and the scenery this time of year is breathtaking."

Being a waitress made me privy to lots of facts and trivia of the area. I knew that Deer Valley Resort was becoming one of the country's most elite skiing areas. It had recently opened in December of 1981 with five chairlifts and thirty trails. Its history could be traced back to 1946 when two residents of Park City resolved to build an authentic skiing facility in the area complete with a mechanized ski lift. Although located only a few miles away from the restaurant, I had never been there.

"I certainly wouldn't want to let Molly down. What time?"

Brad grabbed a napkin and wrote down directions to his house, since it was within walking distance to Deer Valley. "I'll try to duck out of work a little early and meet you at my house at five. Make sure you have hiking gear on."

"Hey, miss, we need more coffee over here." Shrugging my shoulders, I scampered off, my mind reeling with this change of direction in Brad. *Don't try to figure men out*, I scolded to myself.

Clothes were strewn all over my bed, as I tried different outfits on appropriate for hiking. Irritated at myself for making a bigger deal than it was, I settled for a blue flannel shirt, and comfortable jeans. Gathering my hair back into a pony tail, I added small hoop earrings, and a touch of lipstick. Brad had said it would take about twenty minutes to get to his house from Melody's. I was relieved to see Melody on the phone, so I headed out with just a quick wave.

Glancing down at the directions for the third time and making several passes, I was wondering if Brad might have given me wrong directions. "Where is Ontario Avenue?" I muttered. Out of the corner of my eye, I saw a narrow winding road that could have been used as a ski run. "There's no way." But sure enough, there was a sign hidden behind overgrown trees that claimed it was Ontario Ave. Imagining what this road must be like in the winter, I kicked down the gas pedal, and up we climbed.

Brad had described his house as an old miner's shack. A buttery yellow compact house with white trim was perched on the right side overlooking all of Park City. Brad's truck was parked in the driveway. No sign of Randy's car. Maybe I was overly sensitive, but I got the feeling that Randy didn't approve of me. As I neared the house, I could hear Molly whooping and barking, and Brad's deep voice commanding her to stop.

The door burst open and out came a bundle of canine joy, bearing proudly in her mouth a gift of an old slimy tennis ball. Following at a much slower gait came Brad, standing tall with an amused look in his eyes. "You made it."

"Brad Halverson. Where do you live?" Not finding a level piece of ground to throw the ball, I held on to it with the tips of my thumb and forefinger.

It was after five, and the sun had already begun to descend behind the mountains, and shadows were lengthening. "It's got a great view, though, right? I knew Monte wouldn't have trouble climbing that little hill. The winter may be a different story. Did you bring a jacket? It's going to get cool quick when that sun disappears."

Shaking my head, I watched Brad disappear into the house and come back with a well used plaid jacket. "Take this with you. You'll be glad for it in about a half hour." I inhaled the masculine scent of him that permeated his jacket.

Deer Valley was close to Brad's house. Molly had been disciplined well. She stayed by our side until the temptation of water lured her into a faster pace. "Where is she headed?"

"You'll see." With a splash, Molly leapt into the pond and waited with intensity until Brad tossed her the ball. It was a beautiful place. The ski runs cut wide swaths down the mountain in numerous directions. I tried picturing what it would look like covered in snow.

"Wow! That is incredible. Where is the beginner run?"

"You're looking at it." I followed Brad part way up the mountain when he called Molly over in a quiet but stern voice. Pointing to a stand of trees to the right was an enormous bull moose. Stunned, I didn't feel the gentle tug on my shirt, as Brad motioned me to walk back down the mountain. It was my first moose I had ever seen, besides pictures I'd seen. The best way to describe it was a strange looking horse with a huge nose. I felt exhilarated. Molly headed back to the pond, while Brad and I sat on a log bench and watched her water antics.

Brad was right. As the crimson sunset faded to twilight, the air got much cooler. I was glad to have his jacket. Brad glanced over at me, amused. "I can't bear this sounding like a shallow first date question, but I would like to know about you, Grace."

"I had a great childhood, my mother died, my father remarried, and my life fragmented into a thousand pieces." The bitterness that had crept into my voice wasn't the way I wanted to sound. "I'm sorry, Brad. You asked an honest question. But, I guess that is my life."

"The pain of a young girl losing a mother is horrific. It sounds like it still stings. How about on a more positive note? What was a favorite vacation as a child?"

"When I was around ten years old, my parents took our family on a vacation to Disneyland. You can't imagine the thrill that a young girl from the Midwest felt. Seeing the vastness of the ocean, and being together in our old woody station wagon, camping across America; it was awesome."

"California was drawing me, too. That was my destination, to reach the coast, but I passed near Park City and I fell in love with the area. I still have plans to get to California. They just have been postponed for awhile."

"What about your family, Brad?" Molly had rested her head on my shoe, as she rested peacefully after her swim.

"In your style; big family, dad left us, mom was amazing raising a bunch of wild kids, and here I am. How's that?"

My laughing brought Molly back to her feet, searching for her ball. Brad scratched her ears. "No, girl, we have to start heading home." The sun was gone, and the moon was rising clear and bright, making the way home illuminated. There was a peaceful ease between us. A very good night.

# Chapter 27

"Lord, Brad whispered as he gazed into the night sky, shining with millions of stars, "You have named each star. You know me by name, and the number of the hairs on my head. Am I heading in the right direction? Give me a clue on how to proceed, or should I stop right here. I know You love that head strong, beautiful woman. You see her hurt, and You want to give her your peace. But am I the one who should lead her to you? Is this dangerous ground I'm treading on?"

Twisting the door handle, Brad crossed the threshold, to find Randy feet propped up, munching on a triple layer sandwich, watching the news. "Anything good happening in the world, Randy?"

With raised questioning eyebrows he quipped, "No, how about in your world?"

"We had a great time together. She needs a friend, Randy. Don't start in on me."

"Who's doing that, man? You're an adult. You can make your own decisions. Know that I'm here for you, whenever. Brad, you are a huge blessing and a friend to me. You have helped make the transition to Utah easy. Just this morning I was reminded as I read my Bible, that Christ is calling us to love one another as He loved us. That is a tough assignment. Maybe you need to show her real love." Lowering his voice he finished with a grin, "and it helps that the girl is a looker."

Park City was growing. People were beginning to notice the sleepy little mining town that had morphed into a great place to work, play and raise a family. With new houses being built, the work kept flooding in for Brad and his co-workers. He had spent the last few nights working late, trying to keep up with his work load. He admitted as he dashed out of his house peeling a banana that he missed breakfasts at the café. Determined to get home at a normal time tonight, he could start his day tomorrow with better coffee than Randy made. And a prettier face than Randy's for sure.

The autumn breeze sliced through his thin jacket, and Brad realized that winter was crouched, poised, and ready. As he entered the café, he considered asking Grace if she wanted to take a hike in the Uinta Mountains this weekend. The possibilities of many more snow free weekends were scarce.

Securing a table in Grace's section, he waited expectantly for her to appear. Several minutes later she poured him a cup of coffee. Brad noticed she was distracted, distant.

"Hey, Brad. What can I get for you" Her tone was flat.

"I'm thinking some scrambled eggs with lots of hash browns and ham. I've really missed a nice hot meal. You doing alright?"

"Yeah, sure. Yesterday was the tenth anniversary of my mother's death. It's a tough time." She and her sisters had spent some hours on the phone yesterday, reminiscing and shedding some tears. There was also some laughter as they recalled amusing incidents in their childhood.

Katie mentioned to her that their dad had asked how she was doing. "Good for him," she bit back the bitterness in her voice. Shelley ended their conversation with asking her, "So, who is he?"

"Who is who?" Grace had asked startled.

"Whoever it is you went hiking with. It wasn't Melody or you would have said."

"Oh, it's just some guy I met at work. He's a regular. It's no big deal."

"Whatever you say, Grace." I could hear the amusement in her voice.

Brad touched her hand, causing her to flush as she recalled the conversation. "It's alright to feel sad, Grace. Maybe we should take another hike. There is an incredible lake I want to show you. That will get your mind off of other things."

Grace shrugged, "Let me think about it. I wouldn't be very good company. In fact, I won't be good company for a long time. The holidays are coming, and they just are depressing."

"We're going to have to change that. And you let me be the judge of whether you are good company."

"I'll let you know." Grace piled up dirty dishes from the next table, balancing dishes and the coffee pot in a way only those who have waited tables know how to do.

# Chapter 28

Saturday morning broke into song with an array of pastel colors painting the sky. Randy had picked up Melody earlier to go for a bike ride, and I was left with a whole day in front of me with nothing to do. *It's your own fault*, I scolded. Brad never mentioned the hike again, and out of self pity, or just being downright obstinate, I hadn't answered him. Now I was left alone on a beautiful November day. Huddling over a steaming mug of coffee, I plodded outside in my old maroon pair of flannel pajamas. Grumbling at how cold Melody kept the house, I shook my head, wondering how cold it would be this winter. The morning quietness was shattered by the sound of a truck pulling into the driveway. Horrified, I realized it was Brad; I couldn't have looked less appealing. Bending down in a crouch, I hoped to slink into the house undetected. But as Murphy's Law would have it, I heard a cheery greeting, "Good morning, Grace. Is it okay to come in?"

Glancing over at the hall mirror, I saw a frightening looking woman with hair sticking out all over her head. Really, I couldn't have been wearing anything more hideous. It was imperative to either not let him in, or find a way to quickly change. "Uh, well, what did you want?"

"I was hoping you would do me the honor of going with me to a ski swap." He was trying to peer through the window. "Grace, can I come in? It's a little challenging trying to talk to you through the door."

"Can you count to three, and then come in? Then you can help yourself to some coffee." I flew into my bedroom and shut the door just as I heard the front door opening. As I sat on my bed catching my breath, I thought, *what's a ski swap?*

As I came out of the bedroom, looking more presentable, Brad explained that every year at the high school, lots of people exchange their skis for new ones, or try to sell their old ones. "It's a great way for you to get a pair that isn't too expensive at first. Then, when you get better, you might want to exchange them for a better pair next year."

"Wait a minute. How do you know I want to learn to ski, and that I will even be here this winter?"

"You ought to be making up your mind soon. Winter is coming. The hummingbirds were gone from my house about six weeks ago. There may be some truth to the saying that six weeks after these tiny birds migrate to warmer climates, the first real snow falls."

"Maybe I ought to take the wisdom of the hummers and fly home." Brad had found a cup and poured himself some coffee. I refilled mine. "But I guess there's no harm in looking."

An awkwardness filled the room, as we both seemed to realize simultaneously that we were alone in the house. Grabbing my coat hanging on a peg, I headed toward the door. "You coming? Or should just Molly and I go, and leave you here?'

Brad convinced me into buying used skis, boots, poles, and bindings. Never having skied before, I trusted him with my purchase. The place was swarming with people representing every age and size imaginable. Brad explained to me that if I lived in Park City in the winter, I had to ski. Was I staying in Park City this winter? Well, if I did, I had skis and an extremely masculine virile instructor.

November in the mountains could be fickle, and you never could be sure of her mood day by day. The strangely muffled silence that enveloped my room and outside the window, woke me on Monday morning. Shoving my feet into fluffy pink slippers I slapped over to the window and peered outside. "Wahoo!" I shouted. A blanket of white snow covered the ground, erasing any sign of fallen leaves from the day before. In my hometown, this would have been a topic of wild interest in all the coffee shops around town for those adventuresome enough to travel. Here it was merely the first snowfall, with many more to follow. My eyes drifted to the corner of the room where a pair of skis leaned up against the wall. Was I really planning on staying here this winter? It was time to talk to Melody, and figure out if it was even possible to stay.

The house was still dark and sleeping, so I flung on a coat and quietly stepped outside. The cold early morning air was invigorating. The brilliance of the moon and stars above illuminated my footprints in the snow. By the time the intensity of the sun's rays warmed the earth, the snow would be gone, along with my footprints. Right now though, it was a heady feeling being the first one to make a mark on the fresh glistening snow. The air carried the faint smell of chimney smoke. I was reluctant to head back, enjoying this moment in time, but my hands were beginning to feel the cold. Following my footprints back to the house, I reflected on where my footprints were leading me. Melody and Brad believed in a God that could lovingly lead you through each season of your life's journey. I had failed miserably on my own, stumbling and falling, losing my way, heading in directions that only led to empty ribbons of highways.

Welcoming lights greeted me when I pushed open the front door. "Hey, Mel. Have you looked outside? It snowed in the night. Is it okay to ride with you this morning?"

"It's lovely, isn't it? Yes, of course you can ride with me. Just like old times."

After scraping off the car we headed to work. "Melody, when I first got here, you said that you rented out all the rooms in the winter. I guess you were talking about my room, too, right?"

"Well now, Grace, are you thinking about staying through the winter? You are more than welcome to stay. I would have to charge you a little more for rent, but I could give you a deal if you help me with dinner and cleaning up." She swiveled her head, "Does a certain man we know have anything to do with this?"

Swearing under my breath, I muttered, "If you're talking about Brad, well, he's just one of many friends I have."

Melody gave me a vicious grin, "Okay, okay. You don't have to bite my head off."

The 'one of my many friends' wandered to a table, greeting acquaintances along the way. "Good morning, Grace. How do you like the snow?"

Melody looked over at me and winked. 'It's alright," I answered in monotone, glaring back at Melody.

Brad looked at me curiously. "Molly and I want to know if you want to go for a ride after your done working? I'm taking some drawings down to Salt Lake, and would love the company."

Casting a glance over my shoulder at Melody, I saw she was busy taking an order.

"How can I turn down a good looking dog like Molly? I should be done by three." Remembering I didn't have my own car, the realization hit me that Melody would know I was with Brad. Nothing wrong with spending time with a friend, right?

The Chevy truck pulled into the café parking lot, and out jumped one happy dog. Seeing Molly with her tail wagging in sheer joy of life, made me smile. "Hey, girl. Want your ears scratched?"

Brad was leaning against the car door. "Are you still up for a ride?"

"Sure, if you don't mind the smell of hamburgers and fries permeating my uniform."

"Are you kidding? That's every man's dream come true. You may have to fight off Molly, though."

Down the mountain we flew, and I'm muttering, 'me and you and a dog named Boo'. Or named Molly, who did like the smell of the café on me.

# Chapter 29

Grace seemed happy to see Brad when he pulled into the parking lot. But he never was quite sure how to read her. There were moments when he felt a deep connection beginning, and other times she would retreat into her own place of solitaire. "Are you warm enough?"

Grace grimaced, "With a very large dog half sitting on me, I would say I was warm enough."

"Molly, move over here, girl. You're smashing our friend." Brad drug her over closer to him, but within minutes she was parked back on Grace's lap. "Do you have any plans for Thanksgiving?"

"Not really." Grace was not looking forward to the months ahead. If she could will away Pilgrims and pumpkin pie, she would.

A car pulled out in front of Brad, barely missing the front right panel of the truck. Grace screamed an obscenity. Peering over at Brad, Grace taunted, "What? You don't like me talking like that to your tender ears?"

"I didn't say anything." Brad kept focused on the road.

"Yeah? Well, that's just it. You didn't say anything because you are so holy, and you think I am some kind of a major sinner. Isn't that right?"

Brad didn't respond.

"So, you're not going to talk to me?" Grace shoved Molly over and crossed her arms.

Several minutes ticked by. "I'm taking this exit, Grace. Having this loyal mutt between us isn't helping the situation." By turning right off the exit, they passed a sign that read, Sugar House Park. Brad pulled into the parking lot and Molly launched into a frenzied pacing. "Sorry about that. Molly loves this place."

"Molly loves every place," Grace snapped.

As soon as Brad pushed open his door, Molly scrambled out, scaring several birds into flight. Brad walked around the truck to open the passenger door. "Are you getting out?"

"I thought you had to pick up some drawings."

Grabbing her hand, Brad pulled Grace out of the truck. "Let's get something straight. I am not a saint. You aren't a saint. In fact no one is perfect except the One who died on a cross two thousand years ago. I am not shocked by your language, and I don't think less of you because of it."

"You can let go of my hand now."

"Let me get back to my original question." Gently he let go of her hand. "What are you doing for Thanksgiving?" A sudden gust of wind raked fingers through his hair. In unison, they both looked up at the sky. The clouds hung low and heavy.

"Looks like we might be getting some rain down here, maybe snow again in the mountains." They faced each other with the wind becoming wet with rain. His green eyes had an intensity she had not seen before. Brad moved closer and Grace could feel his quick breathing on her cheek. There was a tightening in his chest, and they both were made very aware of their closeness. Grace shivered suddenly and stepped back as the blood coursed through her veins. Brad's fingers tucked a strand of hair behind her ear, never moving his eyes from her lips. His chest heaved, and he blinked as if making his way back from a dream. Molly barked with impatience. Clumsily Brad found the tennis ball at his feet, and hurled it. "Guess we better go pick up hose drawings."

Though the moment had passed, the euphoric feeling remained. Water bulleted the windshield and splattered on the roof of the truck like bullets. The wipers jerked like living things trying to cope with the onslaught of rain. Inside the two humans and one dog stared straight ahead, no one making a sound.

# Chapter 30

Brad was right. The rain turned to snow half way up the canyon. The silence inside the truck must have been an indication that Brad too was deep in thought. I had felt passion before. But my confusion was that besides holding my hand a little too long, nothing really happened, but *something* had happened. By the time Brad had pulled into my driveway, the snow had lessened to a few stray flakes. "Good night, Grace." Brad gave a brief nod. "I'll hold Molly while you climb out."

"Good night, Brad. Good night, Molly"

Melody had left the porch light on. Inside was a note:

*Went to the movies with Randy* ☺

*Where were you????* ☺

*Chicken noodle soup on the stove*

After a hearty bowl of soup, I changed into my maroon flannel pajamas, and crawled into bed. Reaching for the Bible that Brad gave me, I re-read the inscription again:

*To Grace Norman*

*From your good friend, Brad Halverson*

*May you find peace within these pages, and answers to all your questions.*

Okay, Brad. What page do you find the answer to what happened tonight? Hearing the front door creak open, I slid the Bible under my bed. Within minutes I heard a knocking on my door. "Grace, can I come in?" Waltzing in with a broad grin, I knew it would be awhile until I went to sleep.

Melody kicked off her shoes, and slipped into the covers next to me. "I really like him, Grace. We have so much in common. I'm not jumping into anything, though. Oh, I wanted to ask you, what are you doing for Thanksgiving?

Bursting out in laughter, I gasped to get my breath. Melody looked at my quizzically. "What's so funny about that?"

"It appears to be the question of the day. Why do you want to know?"

"For the past few years, I have been going to the high school to serve turkey dinner to families in need. It really is a great time. I was hoping you could come."

"Does Brad by any chance also go to this?"

"He did go last year. Most of us are without family out here, so it's a fun way to share the holiday with lots of people.

The night before Thanksgiving, Melody gave me lessons on baking pies. The heady aroma of cinnamon and apples baking filled the kitchen with scents of fall and Thanksgiving's of my childhood. We were responsible for bringing four pies to the dinner. By the time the pastries were done baking and cooling on the rack, both kitchen and bakers were covered in flour. For the first time in many years, I was excited about the arrival of Thanksgiving.

Before crawling into bed, I threw open my bedroom window to let the cool evening night breezes in. Inhaling the pungent scent of pine needles, I heard a whisper in the wind, *Worship Me in spirit and truth.* A chill inched its way down my body. Shutting the window, I hurdled into bed. *But, who are You*?

Thanksgiving Day bloomed cloudless and exceptionally cold. The remaining leaves on the trees held on with an intense ferocity, as if to keep the full onset of winter from arriving. We arrived at the high school gymnasium along with other food bearing, rosy cheeked neighbors. The flurry of activity and aroma that greeted us put Melody and me in a cheerful mood. Only half listening to the instructions of where in the serving line I was to stand, and how much stuffing each person got, I found myself searching for a particular face. I waved at Carmen and others I recognized from the restaurant.

The mayor introduced himself and thanked all those who brought food and those who were serving. Then nodding to a tall older gentleman, he asked if he would say the blessing. Melody nudged me and whispered, "That's the pastor of our church, Pastor Edwards." He certainly had the voice of an orator.

The room hushed as he cleared his voice and said, "Let's pray." I looked around the room. Most people had their eyes closed. In the corner of my vision, I saw Brad and Randy walk in. A soft glow filled my being. "We are so thankful, Lord, for this special time to count our many blessings. We thank you for that first Thanksgiving many years ago. We are thankful for this one, because we are surrounded by good friends, neighbors, and plenty of food. We give you praise as ***we worship You in spirit and truth***. Amen"

"What?" I blurted out, causing those around me to look at me quizzically. "Melody, what did he just say?"

"Grace, are you feeling alright?" Melody took my hand. "Honey, you're trembling."

Sucking in my breath, I nodded, "Something rather odd just happened. It's nothing." I pushed my hair away from my face. "Hey, we better get to our station. We have some stuffing to serve." For over an hour, we diligently served masses of people. Pumpkins, gourds and cornucopias lined the tables, while an animated community talked and laughed. Randy came by when we were finished serving, and pointed to some chairs Brad had reserved. Leaning near me, Brad whispered with a sheepish grin, "There is a reason why we were late. Molly ate all the chocolate chip cookies I had cooling on the counter. It took us awhile to find a store open to buy more cookies."

Trying to keep the grin out of my voice I responded, "Is she alright? That can't be too good for her."

"Well, she had to make several trips outside . . ."

Something was happening in my heart, and I wasn't certain what it was. A sense of peace was crowding out the space inside where turmoil used to reign. Brad and I spent many evenings together discussing every subject conceivable. Sometimes he would give me verses to look up in the Bible. And sometimes I did. For an early Christmas present, he bought me a ski pass to the Park City Ski Resort. Borrowing Melody's ski clothes, I ventured out, skis in hand, feeling incredibly awkward. I met Brad at the lodge, which was supported by enormous wooden beams, and a fireplace I could have stood in. I would have been perfectly content to sip a hot toddy by the fireplace, but Brad was insistent on teaching me to ski. "But how do you walk in these crazy boots?" I whined while craning my neck upward at the mountain where they taught greenhorn's like me. "And how could anyone call this a beginner hill?" For a moment my panic was forgotten as we watched skiers dancing gracefully with the mountain. They seemed to weave back and forth effortlessly. The snow captured the sun glistening on its smooth surface, catching particles of blue ice, incandescent and brilliant. I felt like I had been transported to a dreamland of white beauty. Then fear gripped me again when I noticed the ski lift whipping around the corner and plopping skiers onto the seat, pulling them up to the top of the mountain, and then swallowing them far away from sight.

"You'll be a natural, Grace." Brad was bending down tightening my already uncomfortable encumbrances they called ski boots. "Put your foot on the ski, yes, like that, and now stomp down." Clamping down with my other foot, I was ready. Handing me the poles, and coaching me as I inched forward, we made our way to the flying chairs. "Wait for it to come to you." Then swoosh, off we went.

The view was enchanting. The towering pine trees flocked with the recent snow, contrasted with the blue of the sky. It was exhilarating. Down below the figures of skiers whizzed by, leaning into their turns. I watched in delight, mesmerized. "Is it a little bit like waterskiing?"

"Similar. Now look up here, Grace. We are about to disembark. Keep your ski tips up. No, not that high. Just so you keep them above that mound of snow. Scoot a little closer and then just ease out of the chair when I say *now*. Ready? Now!"

My guess was that I wasn't ready. Within a second I had tumbled off the chair and onto the snow packed ground. I felt Brad's strong arm lifting me up, wiping me off. It was humiliating to say the least. But the thought that followed was worse. If I couldn't even make it off the chair lift how could I ever make it down that steep hill?

"Lots of people do that, Grace. Don't feel bad. Slide over here. You are going to learn how to snowplow." I looked up into his tender eyes and sympathetic expression, and thought that this man was trustworthy. If he thought I could do it, I would. With endearing kindness he showed me how to make an inverted 'v' with my skis. "By pushing out the back skis, you can control your speed. Like this, watch." Of course it looked easy watching Brad. My skis seemed to want to cross in the front, and not slow me down like snowplowing was meant to do. His relentless patience kept me trying.

"Alright, Brad, I think I'm ready. Here I go." Within seconds I hit the slope with an agonizing halt, while I watched in dismay my left ski sliding down the rest of the hill solo.

Brad appeared alongside of me, concern transparent on his face. "Are you hurt?"

Shaking my head no, he unlatched my other ski, and instructed me to get on the back of his skis and hold on. As we headed down the hill to retrieve my ski, a chuckle started deep in my belly, making its way out to a full out roar of laughter. I felt Brad's shoulders heaving as he tried to contain his amusement. After recovering the errant ski, I rolled on to the snow and let my hysterics run its course. "Brad, I'm not cut out to be a skier. You better give up on me."

"Never. Let's try it again."

By the end of the day, I had figured out the whole snowplowing concept, and had graduated to learning how to glide from side to side. "I'll never forget this day, Brad. You are an incredible instructor. I do believe I'm going to like this. But now, if you would excuse me, I'm heading to the lodge to warm up and rest my aching thighs. Please go enjoy yourself without a rookie slowing you down." Brad took off with agile grace, promising to return soon. Clumping over to the nearest open table, I collapsed into the chair with a groan.

# Chapter 31

Brad knew he was falling, not on his skis, but in his heart. The change he was seeing in Grace made her the more lovable. Was it the determination in her eyes to conquer the mountain, or her childish laughter as she rolled in the snow? Somewhere along the way though, he knew he was smitten. Daily he prayed that she would surrender her heart to the Lord. If he could just put into words the amazing gift of salvation. Prove to her that God loved her unconditionally, just as she was. But only the Spirit of God could open her eyes to His marvelous Light.

Not wanting to stay away too long, Brad returned to the lodge to find Grace with her arms folded on the table, and a weary head cradled on top of her arms. Nudging her gently, he softly spoke her name. With a jerk, she sat up erect and exclaimed, "Oh, I think I was asleep."

She swept her hair from her face and rubbed her eyes, while Brad mused, *how I would love to capture this sleepy eyed childlike innocence. To know her before her world came crashing down around her. Before the world and all its temptations robbed her of her youth replacing purity for bitterness, hardness and skepticism.* He took her hand and tried to read her eyes, into her soul. *You are beautiful, Grace. You want so much to love and trust again. How can I convince you that you are adored and loved by your Creator?* For a moment they sat in the pleasure of the moment. Aware of the intensity that radiated from their clasped hands, she withdrew quickly and stood. "The next challenge is to get to my car without poking someone's eyes out with my pole."

"Allow me to be a gentleman, and help carry your skis." Removing his ski hat with a sweeping gesture, and making a mocking bow, he continued, "and then I would like to take the lovely lady for pizza."

"I doubt I would be much company, but if you aren't afraid of me falling asleep in the middle of a pizza pie, I'm willing."

The Red Banjo Pizza welcomed them with enticing Italian aromas, red checkered tablecloths, curtains, and a pool table in the corner. While waiting for the pizza, Brad racked up the balls Handing Grace a cue stick, he gave her the honors to break them. Watching a solid ball drop, she worked on her next one. Eyeing the corner pocket she dropped another, and another. "You've played before." Brad feigned annoyance, waiting patiently for his turn.

"You showed me up skiing; now it's my turn." She continued to knock them in and left one solid remaining. Okay, buster, let's see what you got."

Brad ran the table without slowing down, and then finished the game by knocking in the eight ball.

"Oh, don't you think you're something." Grace stood, hands on hips, dumfounded.

"I spent some time in pool halls, too." Brad grabbed her hand and led her to the table where a steaming "works" pizza waited for them.

After devouring the whole pizza, Brad leaned back in his chair crossing his hands behind his head. "What do you think of me, Grace?"

"What's that mean? Don't get serious on me now."

"I'm just curious. What do you think of me?"

"Well, you are kind, fun to be around, cute . . ."

"And I can fetch? You make me sound like Molly!"

"Okay, let me reverse the question. What do you think about me?"

"You're not allowed to answer a question with a question. But I'll tell you. You've become more than a friend to me. It didn't start out that way. You were a mystery and I was trying to solve it. You are still a mystery, but a special one. One I think about way too much. Just holding your hand touched something inside of me. But it is far deeper than that, and I can't quite explain it. I guess I was just wondering if you felt anything like that for me. Or if I'm just dreaming."

Stuck by a loss of words, Grace twirled her glass of Coke on the table. Frowning, she glanced up at Brad. "There's a problem here, Brad. Or probably more than one. But, let's stick to the first one. I know enough about your faith, that you are supposed to be like minded with someone you have intentions of going past friendship. I mean, God is a priority in your life, right?"

"He is not a part of my life, Grace, He is my life. Not just a priority. So, yes, that does present a problem. But the strange part that puzzles me, is that I sense God has led me to you, and believe me, I have been willing to be led. There is nothing in this world I desire more than to have you share my faith. But trying to coerce you into believing is not what I'm after. It has to be genuine, or it means nothing.

"It's not that I don't believe, Brad, it's just that I'm not ready to jump fully in with both feet. Too many times I've done that and been burned. I've just got to make sure what I'm doing is the right thing. And, that I'm not just doing it to please you, or Melody, or anyone else. Can you understand that?"

"Of course I can. Can I tell you, though, that those blue eyes of yours sometimes just about drive me crazy?"

"And can I tell you, Mr. Halverson, that those green eyes of yours do the same thing to me?"

Brad leaned toward her, cupped his hand under her chin and lightly brushed her lips with his own. A kiss so innocent and yet packed with an intensity that Grace wasn't ready to explain.

# Chapter 32

Night had fallen, and snow was softly falling as we left the restaurant. The street lamps cast a warm amber glow. Park City lay in a glistening blanket of white, which reminded me of a serene setting on a Christmas card. Pools of light shone from the restaurants, and lights of homes dotted the hillside. Pine trees were dressed in a silvery frost. Brad's sturdy, comforting hand was holding mine as we frolicked through the snow, catching flakes on our tongues, like two kids enjoying their first snow fall. Tumbling to the ground, we fanned our arms and legs into snow angels, and with utter abandon, I laughed at the sheer joy of being alive. Brightly dancing Christmas lights splayed across each intersection. I could hear the sound of familiar Christmas music merrily being carried on the cold night air.

It was a long time before I fell asleep that night. It seems whenever something good came my way, doubt would invade that happiness. Caring too deeply for Brad was dangerous. There was no future in this. Yet the image of Brad's tender face crept sweetly into my soul. Was it the man or his faith? Or was his faith what made him the man he was? It had been numerous times now that I had felt this elation being with him. A calming feeling that something was right. People used drugs to find that feeling. From experience, I knew that there wasn't a drug in the world that could make someone experience this. Weren't we all just trying to find happiness any way we could get it? Trying to fill a void, a hole in our heart by getting high or acquiring things, money, popularity, power? Do we overcome loneliness with sex, or pop a pill to be accepted? Could it be that Brad and Melody's faith was just another tool to cope with life? They talked about a loving, caring God. Someone that loved us so much, that He sent His son to be a sacrifice for our sins. I wanted to believe. Who wouldn't? By believing, Melody said I would receive eternal life with a Father who will never leave me or forsake me. How I longed to curl up without fear onto a loving lap, being safe in strong hands that would protect me, take care of me. Certainly hands that created the Universe were capable of caring for me. But was it true? Brad talked about opening my heart up to Christ, and then having His Spirit live within me. The possibility of experiencing an unexplainable peace and joy just seemed too easy.

"God? If You are real, I sure would like to know it. I guess in a way I have believed in You, because most of my adult life I have been mad at You. It's hard to believe that You are love when You took my mother from me. But maybe it all happened so I could see my desperate need. I don't have a problem admitting I am a sinner like the Bible says. It seems important that I clean up my act. But Brad and Melody, I think You know them, they said I could come just the way I am, and that You would start a change in my heart. Well, I do need a change of heart. I need forgiveness too. I was told that if I tell you that I've done some pretty nasty things that you will forgive me. Will you? How do I know that You even hear me? Or care?"

Pulling the warm covers up to my chin, I reprimanded myself for allowing the swirling notions going on in my head to affect any rational thinking. *You sound like an idiot. Think about this some other time. Right now you have to get some sleep.*

***I have loved you with an everlasting love.***

My eyes jerked open. It was that same thing. How do I describe it? Certainly nothing audible, but it was there in the quiet recesses of my mind. Beckoning me. Crawling out from under the blankets, I reached under the bed for my Bible. "Alright. This is supposed to be written to me. So talk to me. I don't know where to look for answers, but Brad said I would find them here. Show me."

Flipping open this mystery book, my eyes landed on, "For he says, 'In the time of my favor I heard you, and in the day of salvation I helped you.' I tell you, now is the time of God's favor, now is the day of salvation."

A slow smile traveled across my face. Outside in the frosty December night, a single star glimmered as new birth flitted inside my heart, hesitantly at first, then boldly emerged, revealing a new life, a child of the King. I can't say that anything tangible happened in that moment, but I knew life would never be the same again. Something had drawn me that was so compelling, so genuine. Fluffing my pillow and scrunching cozily into the flannel sheets, I murmured into the darkness, "Thank You."

# Chapter 33

For many years, Christmas held only a somber reminder that my life was a failure. My sisters faithfully bought me presents, and tried to make the holidays cheerful. The only thing I would bring to the festivities was my sour mood and defiant heart. My father and Victoria gave the perfunctory gift, and out of spite I'd find the nearest trash can and toss it in. Determined to make this year different, I looked forward to embracing the season by first buying gifts. This also was the first year I had some extra money to actually buy something for others. Writing out a Christmas list, I started with Shelley. She had surprised me by announcing that I was to be an aunt sometime in early May. It was a startling revelation, but one I warmed to quickly. It would be fun picking out something for my new nephew or niece. Then of course there were Katie and Melody. With a slight hesitation I also wrote down Brad's name. My mind wandered at possibilities. I'll know it when I see it, I decided. Should I buy a present for my boss at work? Laying my pen down, I fought an invisible battle. Before changing my mind, I wrote down the names: Dad and Victoria.

My second desire was to attend the Christmas Eve service at Brad's church. After the night of what I might call my spiritual awakening, I knew that it was something of such significance that I needed to share it. Melody and I had been driving to work together in the mornings. As Brad predicted, my car did terrible in the snow. Since Melody's little red bug had rear wheel drive with the engine over the wheels, it was able to plow right through masses of snow. Besides that, it had an amazing heater that blasted much desired heat on bitterly cold mornings. The new female renters, Mandy and Brittany, helped with shoveling if any measurable snow fall had occurred. I was finding out that happened quite often.

"Mel, I have something I want to tell you." We had driven in silence most of the way to work, as Melody concentrated on keeping the car from sliding on the icy roads.

"There's something I wanted to tell you, too."

"Well, you go first, then." I was still trying to unravel in my mind what exactly happened that night and how to explain it.

"My parents bought me a plane ticket to come home over Christmas. I'm really excited. I have to clear it with Floyd first. My only regret is leaving you here at Christmas time. But Mandy and Brittany will be staying in the house, so you won't be alone. And my guess is that Brad will keep you occupied most of the time." While she nudged me with her elbow good naturedly, we both watched in dread as the VW started sliding. Hanging on white knuckled, I watched in admiration as Melody corrected the slide and eased back on to her side of the road.

"Nice work, cuz!" All thoughts about my amazing experience to tell Melody were gone. With a collective sigh of relief, we arrived at Mt. Air safe, with me being unusually grateful for the solid ground beneath my feet.

"Hey there!" I spun around at the familiar voice that filled my senses with delight. There stood Brad, a warming strength against the cold.

"You sure are up early. And how did you ever make it down your treacherous street?" Melody gave us a knowing smile and continued into work. I had sidled up next to Brad and felt the safety and security of this robust, fully masculine man.

"The streets got plowed and salted pretty well this morning. Having four wheel drive helps. Glad to see you both made it this morning. I actually only have time for a quick cup of coffee, but wanted to make sure I at least saw you this morning, even if briefly."

The cold December morning lost its chill as his words fluttered in and rested warmly in my heart. I had never known a man like Brad. Although in the recesses of my mind, I realized red flags were popping up all over as I considered any future with him, but my heart said to take a chance. Being near Brad brought a sense of belonging and security. Judging Brad to be a man of integrity and honesty helped to calm my fears. But when I imagined telling him of my past, and the uncertainty of ever having children, it remained foggy and impossible. Forcing down the doubts and negativity, I basked in my new found faith, and the joy of sharing that with Brad.

Simultaneously we both started talking, and then snickered. "You go first, Brad."

"Knowing you aren't too fond of church, I realize this is a stretch, but I wondered if you would be interested in coming to the Christmas Eve service at our church. It really is an amazing time and I think . . ."

"I'd love to."

. . . you would really enjoy the Christmas ambiance, music . . ."

"Yes, I'd love to."

"You would? Oh, great! Maybe before the service we could go out to eat. My treat."

It has been said that it takes more muscles to frown than to smile. At the moment I knew it to be true, as I felt a smile easily inching its way across my face. "I would love that. And Brad? I want to tell you something, but I want the setting to be right. Will you come over for dinner tonight? I can't brag on my culinary skills, but I'll try to make something palatable."

"Can't turn down an offer like that. I should be off work about five. I'll change clothes and be over by six. Will that work?"

Brad got a coffee to go, and headed back to his truck, stopping at the doorway to wave before vacating it. Leaning on the counter I watched him go. Melody flitted past me with a twinkle in her eye. "Better bring your mind back inside. You have a party of six waiting. I gave them a menu, but they had the look of needing coffee fast. Grace, something has changed between you and Brad. I like it."

Pulling out her order pad and pen she disappeared to her section. Recalling my first days at Mt. Air, I had to admit a lot had changed in my heart toward her, her friends, Brad, and especially God. I would miss the camaraderie with Melody when she started working at the ski resort, after she came back from her Christmas vacation. She'd often cover my back when I'd get behind. I planned on telling her and Brad tonight about my new found faith, and knew that she would be just as thrilled as Brad. It was simply amazing how all this had happened. The bitterness that formulated my life was dissipating into a softness that hadn't been revealed for some time.

On the way home I explained to Melody my plans for dinner. "I guess I should have asked you first. Are you okay with Brad coming over?"

"A free meal with two of my best friends? You betcha!" The two renters weren't often around, but I would make plenty in case they showed up. All day I pondered what I could make that was easy but would taste good too. Tacos seemed to be the easiest solution. I could at least fry some hamburger and cut up lettuce and onions. Mentally, I made a list of everything we would need for dinner. "So what's the occasion, Grace?"

"Just wait and see. I think it will be a nice surprise."

# Chapter 34

All afternoon Brad had found himself gazing out the office window. As he watched a few flakes drifting down outside, he memorized that morning seeing Grace with her rosy cheeks, her blonde hair styled in a thick French braid, twinkling blue eyes in the frosty morning air, and the way he felt when she leaned close to him. He was pleasantly surprised when she had agreed without hesitation to go to the Christmas Eve service with him. "Hey, Brad. Don't forget those plans need to be done by this afternoon. I'm trying to figure out what you find so fascinating outside today." His co-worker, Dave, was grinning at him. "It doesn't have anything to do with a certain waitress over at the café does it?"

"I'm about done with the plans. If a certain waitress did come to mind, I wouldn't tell you." Chuckling, Brad crumpled a piece of paper and tossed it at the wastebasket. "Maybe I'm also thinking tomorrow might be a great ski day."

Finishing his work, he waited for the clock to hit the five o'clock mark. Loading up his back pack, he whistled "Bette Davis Eyes" that had been churning in his head since he heard it that morning. *Lord, I'm afraid I'm smitten. I want to go slow, realizing that Grace doesn't share my beliefs. Would You give me some direction in this? I need Your guidance.*

The snow was still gently falling when he pulled into Melody's driveway. Through his headlights he could see the windows etched in frost, and a flurry of activity inside. Smiling, he zipped up his green ski jacket, and smoothed down his wind tossed hair.

Pressing the button by the door, he heard the doorbell chime inside. And there she was. Face heated and looking a little flustered, she grabbed his hand and pulled him inside. "I hope you like Mexican food." Grace flew to the kitchen and yanked open the oven door. A tantalizing aroma filled the kitchen as she pulled out a steaming apple pie. Headlights flashed outside as a car slowed. "Oh, Melody's home with the ice cream I forgot." Grace concentrated with a quick, no nonsense demeanor. She looked like a young girl as she set the table and filled the water glasses. Brad's heart surged with a budding love for this woman who was capturing his heart. Melody flung open the front door and emerged with ice cream in hand. "Hi, Brad. Good to see you. You know what we need? A warm fire. Would you mind starting one? The temperature seems to be plummeting."

Within minutes a cozy crackling sound came from the living room, and Grace yelled out brightly, "Come eat!"

After dinner and dishes had been cleared and stacked, Grace beckoned her two friends into the living room. She brought out a tray of steaming coffee, and set it down. Standing with her back toward the fire, Grace cleared her throat. "I wanted to thank you both for your prayers for me. Mel, when I first arrived here, I have to admit I thought you and Carmen were strange with all your religious talk. But I soon realized that it wasn't just talk. You really believed it and lived it. And you, Brad. I haven't known too many kind men in my life. You certainly were different. Then you bought me a Bible, which I have been reading off and on. You and Mel guided me to a Peace that I had never experienced. Well, what I am trying to say is, I did it! Last night, in my bedroom. It doesn't completely make sense to me. I still feel so undeserving. But from what I'm reading, it isn't my goodness anyway."

Melody jumped up from the couch and gave her a tight hug. "Grace! That's wonderful news. You will never regret your decision.

There is definitely a party going on in heaven." Grace gave her a hug back, and then found Brad's eyes across the room. Melody's eyes danced from Grace to Brad and back again. "Well, kids, think I'll go do laundry or something."

The fire's light flickered with an amber glow. Warmth crept through Grace's body as she melted into a pair of emerald eyes. "Brad, I didn't do this for you. I mean, it didn't happen because I wanted to please you. I was compelled by a force I couldn't resist. Do you understand?"

"Yes, I do. I see a peace in your heart that wasn't there when I first met you. You're beautiful, Grace." Brad closed the distance between them. Grace watched as if observing outside of herself while Brad touched her cheek and caressed it with his thumb. The fire hissed and sputtered as tree sap heated up on the log. Grace flipped on the outside light. Together they watched the snow gently falling. Brad pulled her close as Grace dissolved into his broad chest, listening to his heart beat in lively harmony with hers. "Grace," he murmured into her hair. The embrace developed into a hunger with a frantic seeking of warm accepting lips. "I better go."

Grace twisted her head up. "What? Why? Don't you like me?"

Trying to steady his breathing to a normal level he looked at her longingly. "That's exactly why I ought to leave. I like you too much."

"Is there such a thing?" Grace peered at him quizzically.

Brad looked down at her with a boyish grin. "No, but you are putting thoughts into my head that I better cool down outside."

"Oh." Grace drew out the word in understanding. "Brad, I am so happy right now."

Tipping her head back, Brad leaned down and tenderly kissed her crimson lips. "Good night, lovely lady. I'll talk to you tomorrow. Thanks for a great meal, and an even better revelation. This is one night I will not forget."

# Chapter 35

That night would forever be etched in my mind as well. Not sure how to pray with eloquent words, I just thanked God that night for giving me new life, for Brad, Melody, and forgiveness. What a delicious feeling to be guilt free, whole. There was much to learn, but for now I rested on the Rock that never moves or changes. I was anticipating the journey ahead. Realistic enough to know that the path wouldn't always be smooth, but I would never be alone again.

There was a flood of activity as Christmas approached. The kitchen kept warm and aromatic as Melody and I baked cookies to give to our friends. It was fun embracing Christmas with buying gifts, and purchasing a new outfit for me. Wanting to look my best for Christmas Eve, I splurged and bought a silky red shirt layered under a soft sweater trimmed with faux fur. Jeans being my only staple, I added a long black skirt, slit at the side, to my purchases. Feeling unusually generous, I bought my sisters several outfits that I thought they would like, and Melody a lusciously warm black and white ski jacket. Trudging to a bookstore, I waded through lots of books until I found a glossy pictured book of the National Parks that were within a day's driving distance of Park City, and sent it to my dad and Victoria. A peace offering, I hoped. Brad's gift was harder to find. I wanted so much to buy something that would tell him how much he meant to me. Wandering through store after store was discouraging. It had to be something special. In an antique store on Main Street, I found an antique drafting tool set enclosed in a leather case, for the architect in him, and in a quaint art gallery next door, a framed painting of a skier soaring down a snow powdered mountain, for the fun loving boy in him. Pleased with all of my purchases, I was prepared to launch into the Christmas holiday with all the glistening joy and mirth of the season.

Although work at the café became more demanding as vacationers invaded the small ski town, Brad and I found time to get in another ski day after nearly a foot of snow fell the previous evening. Still hesitant, I was feeling more confident than the first time out. The world was magically dressed in white, with skiers arrayed in bright colors from all over the world. Even with multiple warnings, I was still in awe at how much snow could fall in such a short period in this winter wonderland.

Tears unashamedly ran down my face when I said good bye to Melody as she headed to the airport. The animated vivacious woman who had irritated me at first, had turned out to be an exceptional friend. Even with two other renters in the house, it wouldn't be the same without her happy chatter and companionship. And being without her to share Christmas would seem like something special was missing. I didn't know at the time that it would be much longer than I would have ever imagined before I would see her again.

# Chapter 36

There was an excitement and anticipation in the air as Grace carefully dressed for the Christmas Eve service. Curling her long hair to frame around her face, she also added a touch more makeup than she usually wore. Adding the sparkling earrings that Melody had bought her for Christmas seemed to complete the image she hoped for. Skipping into Melody's room to view herself in the full length mirror, she nodded in approval. *Brad said I was beautiful. I hope he won't be disappointed.*

Brad met Grace at Cisero's, a local favorite for Italian cuisine. The snow was just starting to gently fall, although the weather forecast was calling for a winter storm warning later that evening. Electricity was in the air as the town was lit up in all its holiday glory. Christmas Carols were being piped in throughout the city. "How utterly magical," Grace smiled as she lifted her face heavenward and felt the snow leave small wet patches as it melted against the glow of her countenance.

"Yes you are." Emerging from the darkness, Brad leaned against the lamp post with a look of admiration. "How lovely you look tonight, Grace. I am honored to be the one taking you to dinner tonight." Hand in hand they entered into the warmth of the romantic Italian ambiance of the little bistro. Checkered red tablecloths and candle lighting only increased the overwhelming sensations of the enchanting evening. Brad was wearing a green and silver striped tie, the first tie Grace had ever seen on him.

"What a handsome man you are, Brad Halverson." The glow of the candle shimmered in their eyes as they reached for each other's hand across the table. *This is what it feels like to love a man,* Grace thought. *So different than anything I have ever known. I am so thankful for this chance to be with him.*

The waiter's interruption broke the spell momentarily. Brad realized that being pulled from those sapphire eyes to concentrate on the menu cooled the room dramatically. *Thank You, Lord, for bringing Grace into my life. Help me to treat her with respect and to never hurt her. Show me Your will for this relationship. I feel so much like a novice in all this.*

After a hardy feast of lasagna for Brad, and butternut squash ravioli for Grace, they left content and ready to embrace the winter blast. Outside the deep moan of the wind rustled through the trees. Grace realized that this land was a hard, beautiful world, invigorating, chilling, and infinitely vast. A chill ran through her body, not sure if it was totally due to the cold or a menacing foreboding in her soul. "Will you be alright to drive, Grace? It really feels like a storm is on its way."

"Of course. Monte and I will meet you at the church in a few minutes." Kissing the top of her forehead, Brad watched as her taillights disappeared in the night before heading toward his truck.

Approaching the church, Grace was delighted to see the flickering glow of luminaries lined up on each side of the sidewalk. Festive Christmas trees were lit inside and out. Huddled against the cold, a steady stream of humanity scurried to the warmth of the welcoming doors. Grace merged into the crowd with trepidation. She tried to dredge up a long ago memory of the last time she was in church. She recalled a young innocent girl clutching her mother's hand at Easter time. Dressed in a yellow pastel hoop dress, with a yellow bonnet to match, she and her two sisters giggled and cajoled with extra energy from jelly beans earlier consumed. *It's been a long time since I've been to church. I feel like I have a neon scarlet letter flashing on me, saying I don't belong here.*

"Grace! Over here." Faint with relief Grace elbowed her way through the jovial crowd, until she latched onto Brad. "Gracie, hey, what's going on?"

Clutching tightly to Brad's arm, she shook her head. "I don't think I belong here, Brad."

"What are you talking about? What's going on? Here." Grabbing her hand, he led her out of the foyer and into a small office area where it was quiet. "Now tell me what this is about."

Staring down at her new shoes, she whimpered, "No one would want me here if they knew my past. You wouldn't want me here if you knew my past. I just feel so ashamed"

"Grace, look up at me. There isn't one person in this church tonight or ever that hasn't done something wrong or that they regret, including the guy you are looking at. At the cross there isn't condemnation, but forgiveness. When you realized your need for a Savior, your sins were forgiven, past, present and future. It's a promise. I don't know all you've done. I don't want to know. But there is One who does know everything, and loves us anyway. You belong here just as much as anyone else. These aren't Brad's words, they are God's. Now, bring back that gorgeous smile and let's go worship the Child who was born in a manger, that we might have abundant life in Him.

As people filled up the church building, Grace felt peace return as she watched people continually stream in of all shapes and sizes, various ethnic groups, old and young, embracing this sacred moment when hearts are stirred, hatreds and jealousies are laid aside, and the miracle of the birth of a Savior is remembered. Grace felt as she sang the joyous carols that she could almost hear the angels singing along with joy at the miraculous Christmas story.

Brad held her hand tightly. The room was glowing with countless candles, spreading their light over rows of red and white poinsettias.

Gold ribbons shimmered from wreaths, hung from each window. Grace closed her eyes and breathed it all in. When Pastor Edwards concluded his message, the ushers lit their individual candles to the main candle, and so in turn used their candles to light the beginning of each row. When everyone had a lit candle the room was hushed by the intense beauty of radiant faces reflected by the light of each candle. In a cappella, the church body sang together "Silent Night" with reverence and meaning. Brad placed his arm around Grace as he watched tears glimmer down her face unheeded. The room was full of love and adoration. It was a night of wonder.

Happy faces and wishes of good will and merry Christmas reverberated throughout the foyer as Brad and Grace headed for the door. "Oh Brad, thanks for inviting me, and reassuring me tonight. I loved every minute."

"Thanks for coming. You being here made it even more special for me."

A tall middle age man tapped Brad on the shoulder. "Brad, could I get your help for a minute? Sorry if I am interrupting anything. I just need a strong man to set the podium and chairs back together, and do some quick straightening up."

"Sure, no problem. Doug, this is my girlfriend, Grace. Grace, this is a good friend and a huge help around church. Tonight he took the role of head usher. Do you have a few minutes, Grace? I'll be back with you as quickly as I can."

*Girlfriend? Yes, I like it!* "Nice to meet you, Doug. Go right ahead, Brad. Let me know if I can help with anything."

Doug reached out his hand and shook Grace's hand. "Nice to meet you, too. We sure could use your help to pick up programs and trash. That would be a big help."

Together they had the sanctuary put together before all of the people chatting in the foyer had left. Brad came over and gave her an affectionate hug. "Thanks. I need to deliver these boxes to the shed and then we should be done. Can you take this money pouch into the office where we were earlier? It is tonight's offering, so put it carefully in the box on the counter. I'll meet you in the foyer in just a minute."

Grace squeezed his hand. Carrying the pouch into the office, she realized that she felt a part of this church already. The last time she had been in this office, she was ready to bolt. *I am accepted, He was rejected. Me, a sinner, and He without sin. Amazing.*

"Hello. I believe you are a friend of Brad's. I'm Doug's wife." A lilting voice matched warm eyes.

"Oh, hi. I'm Grace. What a lovely service."

"Christmas Eve is my favorite time of the whole year. I'm so glad you were able to come. Brad seems so happy lately. It is a blessing that you both are friends. Come on, you two probably want to get out of here. Doug always tries to get everything back in shape, and I'm always ready to get home." Taking Grace by the hand, she flipped off the light and headed for the foyer. "Merry Christmas, Grace"

"Perfect timing." Brad walked over, buttoning up his coat. "Do you want to grab some coffee?"

"I think I just want to go home and savor this whole evening. But I will see you in the morning though, right?"

"I would love it if you would come over to my house as soon as you wake up in the morning. Of course you might have to wait until the snowplows come through in the morning. It is really starting to come down. Anyway, Randy and I have a straggly Charlie Brown Christmas tree, and I want to serve you breakfast for once. The whole time I have known you, you have been waiting on me. I will cook up a feast for a lovely princess.

"Why thank you kind sir. I would love that."

"Call me before you leave, and I will meet you at the bottom of the street. There is no way old Monte will make it up that hill." In the background they could hear the droning of a vacuum. Winking, Brad took her elbow, "Let's get out of here before Doug has us vacuuming."

Heads huddled together, they left in a flurry of snow. Brad brushed off her car. The snowflakes landed on Grace's head forming a tiara looking crown. "My princess," Brad whispered in her ear. "I'll see you in the morning." He mouthed a few more words, but a gust of wind carried it off into the darkness.

With heart pounding, Grace wanted to guess at what those words were. *I love you, to, Brad.* This truly was the best night of her life.

# Chapter 37

The house was dark and bleak when I arrived home. Hearing the phone jingling inside, I wrestled with unlocking the front door. Nobody must be home. Melody would have had the outside lights on brightly welcoming me. Scrambling to the phone, I tried catching my breath before answering the phone. Still mesmerized by the evening's events, I had a hard time trying to comprehend who was on the other end. "Doug?"

"Yes, Grace. I, well we, wanted to know if you could come back to church."

"What? Tonight?" I couldn't believe it. He had to be kidding. Brad wasn't fooling around when he said we better get out of there. "Doug, does it need to be tonight? I just got home."

"Yes, I think you better come. We will see you in a few minutes." Then silence. Now that was weird. Shaking my head, I headed toward the bedroom to change out of my new clothes. Wrestling into my jeans and a warm sweatshirt, I stomped to the front door, swinging on my coat on the way out. Mentally concentrating on the snow covered roads in front of me kept me from trying to figure out such a strange phone call. Sarcastically I thought, what happened, did I forget some trash?

My heart did a drum roll as I pulled into the church parking lot and saw among other vehicles, Brad's truck. *What is going on here?* The momentary foreboding feeling I had experienced earlier in the evening, was coming back in full force. This couldn't be good. Entering the church I heard hushed whispers coming from the same office I had been in earlier. Palpable undercurrent of emotions filled the room. Accusing faces looked up at me. Although I later realized it was only five people plus myself, I literally felt like I was up against an army. Searching out Brad, I saw a look in his eyes that overwhelmed me. Was it disappointment? Hurt? Anger?

Doug moved toward me and put a hand on my shoulder. "Thanks for coming back, Grace. We have a problem here and we were hoping you could clear it up for us. Brad said he handed you the offering bag, and asked you to put it here in this office in this box. For some reason it isn't here. We know there must be an explanation."

"I did put it in here. Wait, your wife came in and we were talking. I might have just laid it on the counter here. It should be here somewhere." I frantically scanned the room.

A stately woman with neatly coiffed auburn hair approached me, wearing dark concern in her eyes. In an authoritative voice she spoke up, "My name is Helen. I am in charge of the finances for the church. This is a very serious matter, Grace. We aren't accusing you of stealing, but we do need to find that pouch."

"Actually, I do think you are accusing me of stealing. I'm different than the rest of you, aren't I? So naturally it would be me who stole the money. Well, I am telling you right now whether you believe me or not, I did not steal the money."

Helen looked me over with disdain. "Then where is it? It couldn't have disappeared."

My face flamed with anger. "I don't know. I thought this was a church that practiced grace and mercy. Well, even in a court of law you are innocent until proven guilty. You hypocrites make me sick." I spun around to find Brad. "E tu, Brutus?"

"Grace, if you say you didn't take it, I believe you."

"But you thought I did before I said anything? So what am I Brad, some kind of a notch in your heavenly belt? What a charming martyr you are, to spend so much time with such a wayward child. All of you. I can't come up with your precious money. It was on the counter. Doug, maybe you should accuse your wife? But no, I forgot, she is in the privileged fold, I'm the outsider." I felt sparks shooting from my eyes. "You better call the police. Brad has my home address. I'm going home to savor this wonderful evening. Ha!" I felt eyes full of rueful accusation boring into my back.

Storming out of the room, Brad caught me before I went out the door. "Grace, I know you didn't take it. Please try to understand where they are coming from. It's a lot of money, and they just wanted to know if you knew where it was."

"This is ridiculous. If they wanted to know they could have asked me on the phone. Instead they brought out the National Guard. You and your friends are pathetic." I yanked my arm loose from his grasp. "Don't you dare ever call me again. Merry Christmas."

I was shaking by the time I reached my car. The elation I had been experiencing in the past months had been replaced with a hollowness that was emptier than ever before. My emotions were spiraling downward. Anger had replaced contentment. I had allowed myself to be vulnerable and this was the result. "Never again," I vowed.

The snow began to fall in earnest. Somehow I made it home and set my plan into place. Jerking out my suitcase from under the bed, I flung all my clothes from the drawers and dirty laundry bag. In the bedroom I tossed cosmetics and toiletries into a plastic bag. Hesitating, I dropped my Bible on top of everything and slammed the suitcase shut. Then I checked my purse to see how much money I had. All the money I had spent on Christmas gifts left a paltry sum remaining. It had to be enough. I threw some food into a bag. Besides gas, I wouldn't have to spend much more. Maybe one night in a cheap hotel, but for the most part, I would have to drive straight through. The phone started ringing. If it's Brad, he'll just have to wonder. If it's the police, they will just have to chase me down. Now concentrate. What do I need? A map. I dashed around the house desperately looking for a map. There was nothing even close to a map. Well, most of the way I could stay on I-80. I'd figure the rest out when I got there. Grabbing my coat and some gloves, I headed out the door, dragging my suitcase with me. I hesitated. Dropping everything I went back in the house and started writing Melody a note. After all, she hadn't accused me.

*Dear Mel,*

*Things didn't work out here. Thanks for everything. I am heading home. Whatever anyone says, Melody, I didn't do it. I promise you that.*

*Love,*
*Your cousin Grace*

A splotch of wet tear dropped on the paper, smearing the ink. Looking around one more time, I headed out the door. Spears of ice pummeled my face and for a moment I thought of reconsidering. The echo of the phone ringing inside prodded me forward. The wind picked my hair up and flung it into a mad dance around my face. In such a short period of time, the ice and snow had frozen on my car. Something whispered in my ear that this was foolish. But my pride and fury drove me on.

Sliding down the hill, I reassured myself that once on the highway it would be less daunting. I was wrong. The snow was coming down in sheets, while the wind flung the flakes into a wild frenzy. Staring into the darkness with snow pellets gyrating in a crazy dance was hypnotizing. How long would I need to drive before I came out of this storm? It had taken me over an hour to go twenty miles. The Wyoming State line was coming up and it wasn't kind to winter drivers. I had heard horror stories of how the wind blew across the road causing impassable drifts. "Oh, God," I moaned.

A soft voice whispered in the night, ***"Why are you running away, my child?"***

"Since you are God, you already know that," I scoffed out loud. I was at an impasse. Too late to turn around, and the storm ahead was too daunting. I flashed on my bright lights which only made it worse. Turning off my lights helped, but being slammed from behind wasn't too appealing either. Inching along, not sure what side of the road I was on, I wanted to scream in frustration. In my rear view mirror a blinding light loomed larger and larger. The fear of its enormity was immediately replaced by relief when I realized it was a snowplow. Pulling off to the side, I let it pass, and quickly fell into place behind it. There was such comfort in following a big powerful machine and knowing there was another human being out in this blinding storm. Following behind the wide swath the blades made allowed a little faster pace. Taking a deep breath and relaxing the strain across my shoulders, I tried to unravel where my life was headed. I knew either of my sisters would take me in. But how could life have taken such an abrupt turn? It seemed like ages ago since I was dabbing on lipstick, and preening in front of Melody's mirror in anticipation of tonight.

"God, why would you let this happen? Everything seemed to finally be making sense in my life. Then, betrayal. Nothing's worse." Remembering the look in Brad's eyes made me wince. Don't go there. I flipped on the radio, following steadily behind my life saver. Several miles later, his left blinker flashed on and off as he crossed the highway and headed the other way. Immediately there was darkness and fear.

No lights, no humans, no guidance. I pulled off to the right, hoping I wasn't headed for a ditch. The Eagle's were crooning on the radio, 'Desperado'.

*Desperado, why don't you come to your senses?*
*You been out ridin' fences for so long now*
*Oh, you're a hard one*
*I know that you got your reasons*
*These things that are pleasin' you*
*Can hurt you somehow*

*Don't you draw the queen of diamonds, boy*
*She'll beat you if she's able*
*You know the queen of hearts is always your best bet*

*Now it seems to me, some fine things*
*Have been laid upon your table*
*But you only want the ones that you can't get*

*Desperado, oh, you ain't gettin' no younger*
*Your pain and your hunger, they're drivin' you home*
*And freedom, oh freedom well, that's just some people talkin'*
*Your prison is walking through this world all alone*

*Don't your feet get cold in the winter time?*
*The sky won't snow and the sun won't shine*
*It's hard to tell the night time from the day*
*You're losin' all your highs and lows*
*Ain't it funny how the feeling goes away?*

*Desperado, why don't you come to your senses?*
*Come down from your fences, open the gate*
*It may be rainin', but there's a rainbow above you*
*You better let somebody love you, before it's too late*

I snapped off the radio, and pounded my fists on the steering wheel. "I don't want to be alone! Oh, God, please help me." Tears streamed down my face. "Where are you God? Where are You?"

***"I will never leave you or forsake you."***

"You already have!" My crying turned into sobs. "I hate my life. I hate it." I threw open the car door, and stepped out into the horrifying silence. "Is anyone out there? Can anyone hear me?" There was nothing but falling snow and the whistling of the wind. "Somebody help me!" I trudged through the drifting snow. There was nothing. Then oomph, I ran into a metal road sign. Only revealing a few letters, I shook the sign as hard as I could. As the snow drifted down, I could make out, "Rest Area 3 miles".

My sobbing turning to hysterical laughing, "God, please just get me to the rest area."

Brushing off the snow with the sleeve of my jacket, I hopped back inside my car, determined to make it three more miles. Shifting from drive to reverse, I rocked my way out from where I was parked, spinning my wheels. Brad's words of warning floated into my mind unwelcomingly, that my old Monte wouldn't do well in the winter snow. Well, he was right about that, but I did hope he would find out along with the others on the judging tribunal, that they were wrong about me stealing any money.

Never knowing if I was on or off the road, I would crack open my door every few minutes, and peer down to the ground, hoping to get a glimpse of pavement. It was the most nerve wracking three miles of my life. The thought that I could have missed the exit often darted through my mind, until I had convinced my agitated mind that I had. Then off to my right a faint light glowed. I stopped the car right where I was, and hopped out of the car. Using my headlights to guide me, I saw a snow masked sign pointing toward the exit. "Thank you, God." I shuffled a path with my boots in the general direction of the exit, so I could see where to turn. A few minutes later, I had plowed my way through to the snow filled rest stop parking lot, thinking I might never be able to move my car again until spring. Staring down at the gas gauge, I tried to estimate how long my car could run on half a tank. The goal now was to stay warm until morning.

# Chapter 38

When Brad got the phone call from Doug about the missing money pouch, he never considered Grace having anything to do with it. He had admitted to Doug that he had asked her to put it in the office box. But thinking of her radiant face after the service he knew without a doubt that stealing money was the last thing on her mind.

Watching Grace trying to defend herself in front of her accusers tore at his soul. And then when she turned to look at him, he felt like Peter must have felt after denying Jesus. The whole night had been phenomenal until then. But then how angry she had been at church as she shot blue sapphire daggers at him, chin hiked, as she marched out the door. He should have stopped her. He should have explained to her. But what would he explain? That people make mistakes? How tender and vulnerable she was as a new believer. She had felt enough rejection and pain in her life.

After calling multiple times, he had headed to her house, only to find the faint outline of tire tracks leaving the house. Where could she have gone? As he was backing out of the driveway, headlights blinded him from his rear view mirror. Heart thumping, he threw his car into park, leaping from the truck, only to realize it was the two renters coming home. Mandy and Brittany merged from the car chirping Merry Christmas. Their greetings sobered as they saw the concern and distraction written on Brad's face.

Mandy, a tall athletic girl, who was enjoying a winter in the West from New Hampshire, clamped a hand on Brad's shoulder. "You doing alright? You sure don't look like you are in the Christmas mood."

Brad, raking his hands through his hair shook his head. "Have you seen Grace?"

Brittany shivering in the cold answered, "Let's go inside. We can talk in there where it is warm. Maybe she is inside sleeping."

Stomping off the snow from boots and shoes, the three crossed the threshold, flipping on lights as they went. Brad already knew in his heart that Grace wasn't here. But where could she have gone in this storm?

Mandy brushed the snow off of her coat, and laid it over a kitchen chair. "Can I make you some coffee? I'm going to make some for myself."

"Would you mind if I looked in her room? If she isn't there I need to go looking for her."

Brittany looked at him quizzically. "Don't tell me you two quarreled on Christmas Eve?"

Eyebrows drawn tight together, Brad groaned. "I'm afraid it is much worse than a simple quarrel." With long swift strides Brad crossed the room to Grace's bedroom. It was obvious at first glance that the room had been emptied of most personal items.

Leaning against the doorframe, he inhaled deeply. "She's gone. But I can't believe she would go far in this blizzard. I'm going out to find her."

Brad s jaw was set in a grim, hollowed expression. Both girls watched his back as he disappeared into the night, knowing they couldn't stop his determined mission.

# Chapter 39

Dawn had not yet tinted the eastern sky, when I was startled awake by a light tap on my window. It had been a long frighteningly cold night. When the frigid biting air became too intense, I would turn on the car and blast heat for as long as I dared. Never in a deep sleep, I often thought I heard holy whispers of comfort and peace throughout the night that would warm my soul, if not my chilled body. Now I sat staring at kind eyes nearly invisible beneath a knit cap and peppered beard. I tried to orient myself to where I was and who this man was. Giving a quick check at the lock button on my car, I felt reasonably sure by some unknown source, that this man was friend not foe.

Crinkled warm eyes greeted me. "Good morning!"

Hesitantly, I rolled down the window several inches, not wanting to let any warmth from the car escape. "Hello."

"This might be a silly question, but what in the world are you doing here?"

Tentatively opening my car door, I unfolded my stiff legs and looked around. From the dim morning light I scanned the vast sea of white. The sun was just beginning to peek over red rock walls on my left. Looking behind me at my car I shuddered in horror. The tires had completely disappeared under several feet of snow. It looked like I had emerged from a casket of white.

"It's not a silly question, sir. The only silly thing about all of this is me. Whew. What a night." Slowly the happenings of the night before enveloped me like a dark abyss. A shiver ran down my spine as I realized how drastically my life had changed in the past twenty four hours.

"My name's Mike." A heavily gloved hand reached out to shake mine. "You don't know me from Adam, but if you can trust me, I can take you to my home where my wife would love to fill you up with hot pancakes and coffee." Looking past his kind face, I saw a heavy duty truck that looked like it had plowed a deep path all the way from the exit. "You won't be going anywhere for awhile, and it looks to me like you might need some friendly company. I think you might like to hear the story of why I'm here, and how I found you."

"Looks like I don't have much choice. I sure hope you are telling the truth about your wife and pancakes, because I can just about smell them from here." I grabbed my purse along with a few essentials, and trudged behind him following in his tracks. With the rising sun, the snow glistened like brilliant diamonds. The calmness after the storm was astounding. I lifted my face to the warming sun and silently thanked God for keeping me safe. Although I felt utterly helpless and saddened by my circumstances, I knew from the promises throughout the night that I wasn't all alone.

As we neared a red brick rambler, the front door flew open to reveal a charming round face and sturdy body, waving a spatula in the air. "Where have you been you rascal?"

"That's Ma." Mike's face softened as he watched her plod toward them. "And you know, I never asked what your name is."

Ma came over and yanked opened the passenger door. "Well, now, who do we have here? Step down, and come warm yourself up inside."

"My name is Grace."

"Wonderful name! I don't know where Pa picked you up at, but come on in, and tell me your story."

My stomach growled in response to the delicious aroma of bacon frying that hit my senses as soon as we entered their cheery home. A fully ornamented Christmas tree brightly blinked in the corner of the room. On the mantle an old manger scene lay displayed with real hay strewn around the cattle and sheep. Immediately I felt at peace. A thick well-used Bible lay on an end table with reading glasses perched on top.

"Merry Christmas to you my child."

My heart lurched as I recalled the plans that Brad had made to serve me breakfast this morning. An image of his strong lean body wielded its way into my mind and the soft brush of his lips on mine. Lifting my fingers to my lips, I glimpsed Ma giving me a knowing look.

"Sit down, child. Fill your tummy and empty your head of any painful memories for now."

Astonished, I counted three plates set out along with three juice glasses at the table. "Were you expecting someone?"

Smiling behind secretive eyes, she nodded, and lovingly pulled her husband over to the chair at the head of the table. "Pa, will you thank the good Lord for our guest, and for this beautiful Christmas morning."

Mike bowed his head and spoke with such tender grateful words, that I found tears forming in my eyes before the prayer was over. After breakfast, Ma gently drew me over to the couch, and coaxed, "You tell us your story and we will tell you ours. Deal?"

Like a dam bursting at the seams, I spilled out my life right up to the present. With the back of my hand, I smeared the tears from my eyes. "Everything seemed to be going so well, until last night when I realized that I would never fit in. I couldn't believe the way those Christian people treated me like a criminal. The look Brad gave me told me everything I needed to know. But you see, I don't deserve Brad anyway. He will someday want children, and I probably will never be able to have kids, so it is better to leave it like this."

Mike stood up and headed for the closet, zipping up his warm winter coat, and tugging on his gloves. Soon the sound of a metal shovel scraping the sidewalk drifted into the house. Ma patted my hand then headed for the kitchen, bringing back the pot of coffee for refills.

Pouring the hot black coffee into my cup, she exhaled slowly. "You are young in your journey, child. People will always disappoint you. We walk through this life with many good friends and companions along the way, but they will disappoint us eventually. Life can be harsh. Jesus never promised us a life without pain. But He stands by us, and shapes us into the people He wants us to be. I know He is guiding you and will for the rest of your life. Now let me tell you a short story. This morning Pa and I woke up to the phone ringing merry greetings from our children. We have been so blessed with precious children, and lovely wide eyed grand children. But for a moment this morning, we gave in to sadness that because of the storm we weren't able to travel last night to be with our loved ones, to experience the wonder of Christmas through the eyes of these little ones. As Pa read the Christmas story we were struck anew at the indescribable sacrifice our Lord gave to us when He humbled Himself at Bethlehem, and took away our sin and guilt at Calvary. Soon we were singing old favorite Christmas carols, and praising God for His love for us. Then Pa cocked his head and gave me a strange grin. He told me that a child outside of our family was in need, and he had to go help her. Then he told me to set an extra table setting because we were going to be with family after all. Now Gracie, I don't know how he found you, but I do know that the Lord is watching over you. I am so glad you are here to celebrate Christmas with us."

With that said, Ma disappeared into the back rooms and came out with a flushed face carrying gaily wrapped packages. She arranged them around the heavy laden Christmas tree. "Come help me dear, to get the stuffing ready for the turkey. We may never spend another Christmas together again, but today you are my daughter, and I will be your mama."

Mike came in later stomping his feet, and shedding his heavy outer clothing. Looking over at me he announced, "Soon those county and state boys will get the highways plowed out, and will be clearing out your rest area. After dinner we will go rescue that car of yours."

"Thank you so much for rescuing me. Ma was telling me what happened with you this morning, but she didn't say how you knew to come find me."

Mike's eyes lit up with a twinkle. "You just listen to the Spirit, Gracie. Just listen to the Spirit." I will never forget that Christmas for as long as I live. Ma insisted that I open a present she had intended to give her daughter. It was a beautiful soft blue sweater that she had knitted. It was amazing that it fit perfectly. Another present she had bought for her son-in-law that she now shoved in my direction held a beautifully detailed atlas of the United States.

"You won't believe this, well maybe you will, but I don't have a map with me. I was going to just guess how to get home. This is perfect. The last gift I opened was a small devotional book comprised of God's promises from the Bible. Flipping through it, I knew I would cherish it and remember always these dear people who helped me through a difficult situation, only to assure me that the God I had chosen to serve was truly a refuge in any storm we might face.

I spent the night curled up in a child's bedroom which once was inhabited by the daughter of this precious woman I was allowed to call my mother for one day. God had brought us together to change what could have been a sad Christmas for all of us into a day filled with laughter and love. As I drifted to sleep under a homemade quilt, I thought about Brad and what he might have done this Christmas. My heart ached for what I left behind. I also knew the road ahead would be a difficult journey. But one thing I did know. I would never be alone.

The days seem to hover, without moving on. The emptiness in my heart matched the emptiness of the miles, and would not leave. It gathered strength like thunder, deepening until the weight of sadness seemed unbearable. After I left the warmth of the Christmas house, the cold seemed to seep into the very marrow of my bones. With the roads still icy in spots, and some drifting from the wind, I traveled slowly. Perhaps more slowly than necessary, knowing that each mile took me further away from the man who had so easily secured a place in my heart. As the winter bleakness of Nebraska merged into the frozen farm fields of Illinois, I longed for the rugged mountains of the West.

In a small town outside of Chicago, I gathered all my change as well as my courage, and called home. Katie answered on the second ring.

"Grace! Where are you? We have been so worried. Melody called and told me you were on your way home, but when we didn't hear from you . . . and then your friend Brad has been calling every day, several times a day. What's going on? Are you alright?"

Closing my eyes, I pictured Brad with his piercing green eyes full of concern. A face I had grown to love. Memories of walks together and the first time he held my hand drifted through my mind.

"Grace?" An anxious voice next to my ear brought me back to the frosted phone booth.

"I'm sorry for worrying you and Shelley. That was wrong of me. If it's not going to be a problem, I would like to stay with you, at least until I get a place of my own. Would that work?"

I felt the warmth of my sweet sister's voice through the phone line. "Of course, Grace. When can I expect you? I'll go make up the guest room right now."

In my heart I wasn't ready to resign to the fact that I was going home. It felt as if I was stepping backwards not forward. Although I could have made it home by dark, I decided to give it one more day. "I should be there by tomorrow sometime after lunch."

After hanging up, I sank to my knees. The cold and the sadness crept inside my very being. A rapping on the door of the phone booth jarred me back to reality. A woman of full girth and an impatient frown on her face, tapped on her watch, "When are you going to be done? It's freezing out here."

I spent the night in a cheap motel that's only boast was that they had air conditioning. Lying in a strange bed, in a strange town, left me feeling, well, strange. The events of the last day ran through my mind over and over. Things I could have said, should have said, kept stomping through my mind. I found myself praying that the truth would be found out. By one thirty my restless and dejected mind sought for peace. Flipping on the light, I yanked open the nightstand drawer and pulled out the Gideon's Bible. When you are lonely . . . Isaiah 41:10

> *So do not fear, for I am with you;*
> *do not be dismayed, for I am your God.*
> *I will strengthen you and help you;*
> *I will uphold you with my righteous right hand.*

I spent some time in prayer, asking God to go before me, to guide me. I felt strongly that he had brought Ma and Pa into my life to reassure me that He hadn't forgotten me. His strength was sorely needed for the days ahead. Then my prayers were directed toward Brad. *May he find a special woman to give him children, and someone that shares his beliefs.* The choices I had made in the past would haunt me for a lifetime. Yet I had been told that I was forgiven completely. Taking the Apostle Paul's advice to forget what is behind and strain toward what is ahead, seemed like the best thing to do.

Counting out the last of my money, I filled up my tank the next morning, and poured some thick gas station black coffee into a Styrofoam cup, and headed out on my last leg of this impulsive journey. Thankfully, I had not encountered any more bad weather, and amazingly my old Monte hung in there, like a faithful friend.

# Chapter 40

The warm love and embraces from my sisters cheered my soul. As soon as I arrived home, I knew that the defiant self centered girl that had left was not the same as the one who was now blabbering to Katie and Shelley about my trip. Trying to keep my voice buoyant, I talked about some of the harder chapters, never unveiling the depth of my loss. There was a lot of molding and shaping the Potter still needed to do on this old lump of clay, but I had come a long way, and I was willing to be open and pliable in His hands.

Katie and I said good bye to the past year quietly, watching the ball drop in Times Square from the warmth and comfort of her worn comfortable couch. And now a new year lie ahead with all its unknowns. So much had happened last year that I could only cling to God with all the days ahead. After Katie went to bed, I turned to watch the news. The weather report gave elaborate details of how the west was getting pummeled by another snow storm. Without governing my thoughts I wondered what Brad was doing. He would be loving all this new powder for skiing.

Throughout January Brad continued to call, but the amount of his calls lessened each week. Each time he called, Katie would look over at me, the phone dangling in her hand, with raised eyebrows. Always there was that moment of hesitation when her questioning look waited for my answer. I could have easily grabbed the phone and heard the sound of his voice, knowing my heart would fragment into a thousand emotional pieces. Melody's call had been hard enough. Brad had informed her of the Christmas Eve event, and in her typical perky fashion said, "Grace, everyone knows you didn't take the money. When the cleaning lady came in to empty the trash after Christmas, there was the money pouch. You must have brushed it with your sleeve and it fell into the trash. Everyone feels so bad for accusing you, Grace. Just come back. I really miss you. And of course, someone else really misses you."

"It's not that easy, Mel. I'm not the right girl for Brad. Really. How's Randy?"

"Hey, girl, don't change the subject. Although, I do have to admit, Randy and I are doing great. But there is one sad puppy hanging around town that really misses you, Grace. I don't understand why you are being so obstinate."

"Just trust me that this is the right thing to do. Say hi to all the gang at Mt. Air. I actually got a job waiting tables at a local restaurant here in town. My boss is crabby, though, and the girls I work with aren't anything like you."

"Then come back! You could work at the ski resort with me, and then in the spring we could start working at Mt. Air again. Floyd would hire you back in a heartbeat."

"I can't Mel; you just have to believe me."

"Can I tell Brad you said hi when I see him?"

"Sure, of course. But please tell him I'm doing well. And that . . . well, that I have a new life now."

"Stay out of trouble, cuz. Hope you found a good church. I pray for you every night."

My throat tightened as I choked out, "I love you, Mel. Thanks for everything."

After a few false starts, spring eventually came to my hometown. The first signs of spring, robins pecking for worms in the thawing ground, new born colts and lambs, were augmented with the arrival of my nephew Luke. Shelley and her husband Nate were captivated parents who found that this seven pound wonder had turned their life upside down. Other positive signs appeared, along with the warming breezes and longer days. My boss at work had begun to loosen his fierce angst against me, and I held a more respected position than the new kid on the block.

Brad's letter arrived on a Saturday, when I was feeling particularly lonely. Trying to walk nonchalantly from the mailbox, I felt my heart thundering as I closed the bedroom door behind me.

*Dear Grace,*

*Let me warn you before I get too far, that I am not a writer. Drawing up plans I can do, but putting down on paper what is in my heart is not a talent of mine. So please bear with me, and also know that there is a pile of wadded up papers on the floor next to me that just didn't convey what I wanted to say.*

*Since all of my calls have not been answered, the intelligent man that I am finally had to come to the conclusion that you don't want to talk to me. By now you know that the pouch was found, and need I say, some very humbled people want me to tell you that they are sorry. Grace, I understand your feeling of betrayal, how hurt you must have been. I shake my head even now trying to understand how in one night I experienced the best night of my life only to fall into despair over the worse night of my life. I searched for you everywhere, hoping to glimpse your car somewhere, rescuing you, wrapping you in my arms and keeping you safe.*

*Christmas morning, Molly and I sat in gloomy silence, straining to hear the chime of the doorbell. I do believe that she knew as well as me, that we had lost our special friend and companion. Grace, do you know that Christmas Eve I knew so deeply in my heart that you were the one for me? I never wanted to ever tell a girl I loved her if I didn't mean it. But out of the depth of my soul that night, I shouted those three words which the wind carried away. Do you know I have shouted those three words over a hundred times into the wind, hoping that you might hear the sound of my voice and the longing in my heart on a windy day?*

*Since I left my home number and work number with all the many messages I left, I know that is not why you haven't called me. In my heart of hearts I truly believed you felt like I did, but I'm just a guy, so what do I know? Just know that you can call me anytime. Anytime.*

*Now my advice from someone who honestly cares for you. Don't hold your bitterness in for too long. Let it go. Forgiveness is a freeing act. Without forgiveness, you rob yourself of true joy. I pray for you daily that you won't fall back into the empty lifestyle that had you chained before. You are a new creature in Christ.*

*And finally, those three words that just won't stop churning in my head.*

*I love you.*
*Brad (and Molly)*

With shaking hands I set the letter down on my bed. Pulling and tugging at the ice crusted window, I shoved the window up and stuck my head out to the gloomy afternoon of bare tree branches etched against the smoky gray sky, straining with all my might to hear the words on the wind. Nothing. *It's because I love you that I don't return your calls, Brad. Because I love you.*

The day came when Katie informed me that dad and Victoria had invited Shelley, Katie and me to lunch at their house. "No, thanks," I answered without hesitation.

"Grace, think this through before you say no. They are offering this invitation as a peace offering. Please reconsider before making a decision. I know this isn't easy for you, sweetie. But you will have Shelley and me there right alongside of you."

Oh I knew the stubbornness in my heart wasn't from God. I actually knew somehow that my new found faith was being tested. "He was the one that treated me terrible, Katie. Why should I come back groveling to him at his beck and call?"

"I know it's hard. It isn't easy for me either. After all these years, we still miss mom incredibly, but dad is still our dad. Deep down behind that gruff exterior is a man that wants to make amends. Please at least try this once."

"Let me think about it," I grumbled. This wasn't something I could do on my own. Throughout the day, I threw up a plea to God to help me see my dad through His eyes. And through that still small voice I would hear, *Forgive as I have forgiven you.*

Shelley, Katie and I arrived on a beautiful warm summer afternoon when I could have been at the beach reading a good book. As Shelley pulled up to the familiar colonial home that we had been raised in, a slow churning started wreaking havoc in the pit of my stomach. Noticing the hollyhocks and four o'clock flowers that my mother had once planted in the front yard, sent my head spinning. Entering the house, I took a deep breath. I can do this. My father can no longer dominate me, and I don't need his affirmation to feel good about myself. But when he answered our knock, and I stood before this giant of a man whose blue eyes reflected my own, I knew that I was still intimidated.

In spite of Victoria's warm attempt at hospitality, I felt hostility oozing from my pores. Shelley, trying to cut through the tension in the room, babbled cheerily. Scanning the living room, I sought for something that would remind me of my mother and calm my inner turmoil. There was nothing after all these years. It was as if she and my sisters and I hadn't lived here at all. Pasting on a conciliatory smile, I endured the afternoon.

The car ride home was silent until Shelley quietly spoke, hands firmly gripped on the steering wheel, that it was time for feelings to heal. It was time to mend the past, to forgive. A time for grace.

For so long growing up, I had worshipped at my father's feet as if he were a god. I inhaled his words and philosophies, shrank under his criticism. His approval is what I longed for, and rarely got. Was I still that little girl needing his acceptance? Wasn't he just a man, struggling with right and wrong like we all were? Didn't I now find my identity, not in a human father, but in my heavenly Father, who did accept me, approve of me, and would never reject me? It was certainly something I needed to think and definitely pray about.

It was easier than I had thought to let friends from my past know that I wasn't interested in doing those things of the dark side that used to draw me. After a few attempts of party invitations, they moved on to more willing victims. I found a church I liked and fell into a group I knew Melody would have enjoyed. Always my biggest challenge was squelching unwelcome memories of the time spent out West that left me yearning to go back. When those times of longing would arise, I would remind myself that Brad, although always near to my heart, could never be more than a friend. Often I found myself mentioning him in my prayers; that he would eventually find that woman who could give him children, and love him as he deserved. Once when a black Lab bounded my way, chasing down a tennis ball, my heart lurched with hope, only to realize it wasn't Molly.

Sometimes in my sadness, the moaning deep within in my soul would resound through the breezes, carried on the wind of cool spring air, so that even the birds paused in their jubilant trumpeting in of the new season to listen to the woeful sound. I willed for my heart to embrace spring with enthusiasm which came with the rich clean aroma of rain drenched earth. Crocuses poked through the ground like proud sentries welcoming in the warmer days, as I sought healing by holding baby Luke in my hungry arms.

Examining the path that I have been on, I know without a doubt that my time out west had a purpose. Arriving there as a bitter, angry, young woman, I was shown love and guidance toward the best decision of my life. Not to mention true friendships, an appreciation for God's amazing Creation in the mountains, in His people, and yes, learning to love a man that readily gave back love who will be divinely etched on my mind forever.

His eyes haunt me, and his laughter peals in my ears. His look of disappointment in me is never far from my mind. I am both relieved and grateful that he will always know the truth about that night. But through this I have realized that fellow human beings are not always completely trustworthy, but God has never failed to live up to His word in our relationship. And I know He has a plan for me, and I am willing to see where He leads.

As the fresh winds of spring evolved into the warmth of summer, so did the seasons of my life start changing. Reid Skiles had lost his wife several years prior to cancer. I met Reid at a dinner party of a friend I had met at church. It was apparent from the onset of the party that we had been purposely paired together. He and I realized this pairing at precisely the same time, which left us both feeling intuitively awkward. Without trying to look intentional, I would glance over at him, only to finding that he too was glancing at me. After dinner I excused myself and headed for the porch. Outside the fireflies were dancing in the open field across the street. Warm humid air enveloped my body as I breathed in the scents and sounds of home. A light touch on my shoulder brought me face to face with Reid. With the darkness setting in, it seemed less intimidating to appraise Reid in the shadows rather than by the harsh lights inside. He was handsome in the fact that he seemed genuine and sincere; a man who had experienced his own wounds, and yet remained optimistic. Nearly a decade older than me, our relationship began only as a friendship of two mutual hearts seeking God's direction. After a long battle of cancer, his wife passed on, leaving him to raise their two children, twin boys. Struggling at times with his faith after petitioning to a loving God to bring his wife back to health, he had to do some soul searching, and like me, came back to the One who is faithful and promises to bring us through the storms of life, not avoid them.

Knowing it wasn't fair to compare Reid with Brad, I did anyway. In my thinking, God had sent me Reid with a readymade family. Reid had done well in the business world, a vice president of a packaging company. An intelligent, mature, Christian man, who was satisfied with his family of two boys, just seemed so convenient and right. So although Reid never made my heart race like Brad had done, our friendship was genuine and unfeigned.

But whereas Brad was an outdoor enthusiast, Reid leaned heavily toward art and culture, something I knew almost nothing about. My first experience was to the play, *Les Miserable's*. Reid had planned the night to perfection. Having a sister in town who watched the twins allowed us in the beginning of our relationship many outings alone. I sensed that Reid wanted our time together to be without the distraction of Jack and Jerry, until we got to know each other better.

Without owning anything proper to wear to a dinner and a play, I borrowed a wispy floral summer dress from Katie. She arranged my hair on top of my head, with soft curls that framed my face. Looking in the mirror, I shrugged my shoulders, thinking, *this is about as close to elegant as I will ever get.* Reservations had been made in advance at the Taillevent, a French restaurant which ended up an hour's drive outside of town, close to where we would be seeing the play. If it wasn't for Reid's composed and competent demeanor I may have felt overwhelmed and somewhat intimidated. Reid ordered for both of us in French, no less. Within minutes the waiter returned with two shining glasses of red wine.

"Reid, I know this sounds silly, but I don't drink anymore. I'm afraid I have drunk too much fruit of the vine in my past. I would prefer just water."

"Of course, Grace. I should have asked first. Which makes me realize that I don't know you very well. I see a beautiful woman, with charm and grace, like your name, who I enjoy being with so much. You came into my life when I couldn't begin to imagine having a life outside of the pain of the last several years. Watching my wife slowly dying and not being able to do a thing about it, trying to explain to our sons what was happening to their mother, and crying out to a God who seemed to not care. Somehow we got through it, and looking back I do see God's faithfulness through it all. The boys miss their mother of course, and I admit to being slow witted in trying to be a mother and father to them. My sister has been a godsend, but she has children of her own, and I know that Jack and Jerry can be more than a hand full at times. But life goes on, and we are adjusting. And you, Grace. I sense some sorrow in your life as well. I would love to know you better. I know you lived out west for awhile. What brought you back here?"

Leaning forward, I clasped his hand. His dark curling hair, strong jaw and affable smile all were pleasing but something inside me held back. "Reid, I am so enjoying this night. Maybe some other time we can talk about me. Right now I just want to experience all of this wonderful atmosphere. I have never been in a genuine French restaurant, and certainly never with anyone who could speak French so fluently. I am impressed."

Feeling a bit chagrined as I thought of the restaurant where I worked compared to where we were dining, I tried to remember that as a child of the King, I had nothing to be ashamed of. Reid was a courteous and gallant man, who never made me feel inadequate, and for that he endeared himself to me.

*Les Miserables* was magnificent. I found myself riveted to my chair, inhaling the spectacular scenery, the talent, and how the story line drew me in. When Eponine sang the haunting words of *On My Own,* I closed my eyes and drank in the music, feeling the sting in my eyes.

*And now I'm all alone again nowhere to turn, no one to go to*
*without a home without a friend without a face to say hello to*
*And now the night is near*
*Now I can make believe he's here*

*Sometimes I walk alone at night*
*When everybody else is sleeping*
*I think of him and then I'm happy*
*With the company I'm keeping*
*The city goes to bed*
*And I can live inside my head*
*On my own*
*Pretending he's beside me*
*All alone*
*I walk with him till morning*
*Without him*
*I feel his arms around me*
*And when I lose my way I close my eyes*

*And he has found me*
*In the rain the pavement shines like silver*
*All the lights are misty in the river*
*In the darkness, the trees are full of starlight*
*And all I see is him and me forever and forever*
*And I know it's only in my mind*
*That I'm talking to myself and not to him*
*And although I know that he is blind*
*Still I say, there's a way for us*
*I love him*
*But when the night is over*
*He is gone*
*The river's just a river*
*Without him*
*The world around me changes*
*The trees are bare and everywhere*
*The streets are full of strangers*

*I love him*
*But every day I'm learning*
*All my life*
*I've only been pretending*
*Without me*
*His world would go on turning*
*A world that's full of happiness*
*That I have never known*
*I love him*
*I love him*
*I love him*
*But only on my own*

At the end of the song, I felt Reid's eyes look at me questioningly. He leaned over and whispered, "It is a touching song, isn't it?"

I nodded, wiping tears away that seemed to flow from my heart. "It's so easy to feel her sense of loss."

He smiled and took my hand. "I suppose every young girl can relate in some way."

"Yes, I suppose so."

Reid also introduced me to the ballet and opera. Even with a desire to be an appreciative student in that cultured world, I couldn't truly engage like I know Reid would have wanted me to value the arts. Without warning, I would feel a chortle begin to form in my stomach as I thought of Brad in places like that. It was an understatement to say that these two men were different in numerous ways.

My work hours were very similar to what I experienced at Mt. Air. The breakfast and lunch shift was my favorite, and since those were the least desirable for tipping, I was awarded those shifts and weekends off. Once Reid hinted to me about a job opening at his work for a receptionist position. "Actually, Reid, I really like my job. It is a good feeling to know what I'm doing, and I think I do it well."

"I'm sure you do, Grace. I just thought you might like a job that is steadier with benefits."

"I like my job, Reid."

"That's fine. Just thought I'd offer."

I suggested to Reid that the following Saturday we could all go to Lake Michigan and enjoy a day at the beach. Living in a small suburb north of Chicago, meant living only an hour from the sparkling blue waters of Lake Michigan, and her white sandy beaches. In my mind, I pictured Reid and me walking hand in hand along the serene and spectacular coastline. I could see Jerry and Jack running their toes through the sand and building sandcastles, watching in amazement at my prowess of building moats and turrets on an elaborate sandcastle.

Loaded down with towels, sun tan lotion, snacks, and a dozen other necessities for a great day at the beach, we headed to find a spot on the crowded summer afternoon. The complaining started as soon as Reid picked me up. As I understood it, it wasn't fair that I got the front seat with their dad. The next point of complaint was why I had to go along at all.

Reid parked the car as close as he could get to the beach, which seemed like a mile at least. "Okay kids. Grab something to carry and we'll find a spot to lay our things."

As I started dividing out what each person could carry, I realized the boys were long gone. Sweating, with tiny flies nipping at my legs, I found the twins down by the beach, kicking sand at each other with utter joy. "Hey, you guys. Quit that! You are kicking sand on other people. Just stop it."

"You're not our mother." Jerry quipped.

"Yeah," Jack concurred.

Reid calmly laying out towels and setting up the umbrella, told the boys to behave.

Collecting my cool I suggested we build a sand castle.

Jack rolled his eyes. "That's for kids."

"Well what do you think you are?" Those two were starting to get the best of me. Reid cast a sidelong glance at me. I just shrugged my shoulders.

Although I had seen glimpses of the twins, we had never spent quality time together. They were identical twins, but with unique personalities. Both had their father's curly hair and expressive brown eyes. And they both did not like me.

"Okay. The last one in the water is a rotten egg." I shrugged off my shirt and shorts and ran as fast as I could to the water's edge. When I looked back all three males were looking at me with an amused look.

Humph. Forget them. They were only seven years old after all. The cool water was refreshing. I had always been a strong swimmer, and loved jumping the waves. Before long Jerry, Jack and Reid were in the water laughing alongside me. That's better. Jerry moved next to me with a grin on his face. Smiling back, I commented, "This is great isn't it?"

I felt him touch my back, and then felt a flopping in my bathing suit. He had thrown a disgusting fish we called alewives down my suit. Alewives, a silvery fish about six inches long, are often found washed up along the shore. Somehow Jerry had found a live one, and much to my chagrin, I screamed like a banshee . . . whatever those were.

I can't say that the rest of the day went any better. Reid tried to control the twins, but they seemed determined to make my day miserable. To complete the day, I found a parting gift as I dug in my purse for the house key. I pulled out another alewife, but this one was definitely dead.

# Chapter 41

That night Katie overheard my sighing in mental anguish. "What's happening, baby sister?"

"Those kids! They seem to know just the right things to do or say to irritate me.

Katie plunked down beside me on the couch, draping her arm around me. "What do you expect? Those boys lost their mother not too long ago. You of all people must know how hard that is. They see you as a threat to them. The poor kids feel like they are losing the unsteady ground they are now barely standing on. In their eyes, you might be taking their daddy from them, or trying to take the place of their mommy. They are just little boys dealing with a passel of hurt."

"Okay, Miss Psychoanalyst. What do you suggest?"

"Why don't you bring them over here sometime, without their dad? Show them you care about them. Make chocolate chip cookies, play a game with them. Let them see you as a person without their dad in the equation. You can win them over, Grace."

"Would you be here, too? I'm not sure I can handle them by myself."

Katie patted my shoulder. "Sure, just let me know when. But I think you're underestimating yourself."

When I presented my proposition, Reid smiled and gave me a swift hug. "You're a sport, Grace. I'll drop them off Wednesday night."

With all the ingredients purchased to make cookies, and the board game Clue waiting to be played, I was anticipating making a positive impression on the boys. Katie was right. The death of my own mother was a shattering life experience. How much more so for these young boys who had to watch their lovely mother painfully slip away? I was determined to be more patient and understanding.

That's when I heard one of them, I guessed Jerry, outside the open living room window, inform his father, "But dad, we don't want to go to Grace's house. We don't like her."

Steeling my resolve, I didn't wait to hear Reid's response, but instead pasted a smile on my face, threw open the front door and greeted them with overdone enthusiasm.

Reid looked uncomfortable standing next to his sulking boys. Katie, thankfully, ushered all three into the house with genuine warmth.

"Now I know you are Jack and Jerry, but how do I know who is who?"

"Jack has a birthmark on his left arm that looks like it spells his name. See?" With that information, Jerry wrangled his brother's arm and proceeded to show the birthmark.

"Well isn't that clever!" That's a good thing to know." Katie smiled up at Reid. "We will take great care of these two. Grace is well prepared."

I looked at Katie in amazement. They boys seemed almost angelic in her care.

"Jack", I chirped, "I never knew that about your birthmark."

"You never asked." Jack responded. Jerry made a face at me.

Reid smiled sheepishly at me. "I'll be back around eight. Bye boys. Behave."

Looking over at Katie, his smile broadened. "Thanks for being here to help."

"Oh, I'm happy to help."

As the door closed, I stared over at my sister. Most of my life I had spent being self absorbed. Now I examined Katie as a woman, and not just a sister I was always leaning on. Katie was slightly shorter than me, with facial features resembling my mother, who was quite a beauty in her time. Katie had always been a giving compassionate person, which is why she did so well managing an assisted living facility. As I witnessed those rambunctious boys surround her, chatting gaily, something tugged on my conscience. Had Katie ever been in love? I didn't even know. She would someday be a wonderful mother, and surely make some man very happy.

Gathering courage, I forced a cheery, "Would you guys like to make some cookies?"

Jerry looked over at me with disdain. "That's for girls."

Katie jumped in brightly, "Ah, but boys like to eat cookies. Come on. We need your help."

Chairs were pushed over to the counter while Katie taught the boys how to crack eggs, measure by the teaspoon, and mix in the flour. I watched in horror as batter flew everywhere. The boys and Katie giggled as they heavily sampled the cookie dough. Slumped on a chair, I watched with envy as Katie easily charmed the twins. By the time Reid showed up to pick them up, they were bouncing up and down recalling the fun time they had at *Katie's* house.

Jack pulled on his dad's sleeve. "Hey, dad, I figured out it was Colonel Mustard, in the ballroom, with the rope. Katie sure is fun." I felt like a complete failure.

Dragging myself off the couch after an unusually busy day at work to answer the phone was challenging.

Reid's deep masculine voice on the other end reminded me that he had purchased some special symphony concert tickets for tonight. It wasn't that I didn't like good music, but my idea of a concert was someone more like Carole King, or Chicago. He must have heard the sigh in my voice. "You did remember, didn't you?"

"Sure, but I just got home and I'm wiped out. Reid, to be perfectly honest, I'm not that big on symphonies."

There was a long pause, then, "I wish you would have told me that before I bought them. What do you want to do tonight, then?"

"I don't know. How about a Cubs game? A big juicy Wrigley Field ball park frank with lots of onions, mustard and ketchup sounds amazing right now."

"You're kidding, right?"

"Actually, I'm not."

"Listen, Grace. It sounds like you have had a long tiring day today. Maybe we should just stay home tonight and do something tomorrow. You decide. What sounds fun?"

"Water skiing? Roasting marshmallows on the beach?" I couldn't hold myself back.

"Grace, where are you going to get a boat? What's gotten into you?"

I twisted the phone cord around my finger. "Reid, I have been thinking. I might start taking night classes. Maybe some history or creative writing classes. I knew a guy that took night classes . . ."

"Why in the world would you want to take night classes? What good would they do you? Don't you just want to eventually get married, and stay home and be a housekeeper?"

Shocked, I counted to ten before answering. "That certainly is a possibility, but I'm not married, and I would love to further my education. I feel like I am getting a second chance at school. I kind of blew school off before."

"Grace, don't you know how I feel about you? I have envisioned you being an intimate part of my life someday, of Jack and Jerry's, too."

Sucking in air between my teeth, I tried to get my breathing under control. "Reid, that is really a wonderful sentiment, but it takes two people to complete that picture, and I frankly don't see myself in that role in the near future, or maybe ever."

"Grace, are you telling me that you don't have feelings for me? You don't see a future with me? Maybe we should put this conversation on hold until a later time. I'll call you tomorrow. Good night."

"Good night."

I hung up the phone none too gently. Watching the blue flicker from the television in the other room, I knew Katie must have heard the whole conversation.

"I can't believe how you treat that kind man!" Katie shouted from the other room. A second later an irate woman rounded the corner, hands folded across her chest. "After how he has treated you like a queen and been patient with you, lavishing you with gifts. Do you even have a clue what a wonderful man Reid is?"

"Whoa. Calm down." I put my hands out in defense. "What is going on here?"

"You don't deserve him. If I had a man like Reid who was in love with me I'd . . ."

I stared at her in wonder as she slammed her bedroom door.

"Well, then. So that's how it is."

# Chapter 42

A plan started forming in my mind after that eye-opening night. To make it work, Jerry and Jack would have to be included in my scheme. Getting them to even listen to me might be my biggest challenge. Since they spent their days with their Aunt Susan during the summer, I thought I could start there. As soon as work was over the following day, I drove over to the house, formulating the details as I drove.

Susan was a female version of Reid with the same brown eyes, willowy, immaculate shoulder length brown hair. After introducing myself, she gave me a knowing look. "Reid has told me so much about you."

Having two children of her own, I imagined how chaotic her days must be. "Susan, would you mind if I talked to the boys?"

"Sure, go ahead." Leading me to the backyard, she subtly mentioned the need Jack and Jerry had for a motherly influence in their lives.

Together we watched as a twin dressed as a cowboy ran past followed by an Indian holding a tomahawk. "Please tell me that's not real," I mumbled under my breath, picturing my blonde hair becoming a much desired coup.

"Hi, boys. Um, can I talk with you both for a minute?"

"What are you doing here?" That was from the cowboy.

"I just thought I could talk to you, Jerry. I think you both might like what I have to say."

"I'm not Jerry."

"Okay, can I just have your attention for a little bit?"

"What did you bring us?"

"I brought you a plan to get rid of me."

Both the cowboy and Indian stopped in their tracks and stared at me, then said in unison, "How?"

"'How' to you, too." By now I was pretty well convinced that these boys did not want me as their motherly figure. "I believe that your father and I aren't really suited for each other. He is a wonderful man and a great daddy to you, but I have an idea of someone that is much more compatible with him than I am."

"What does capible mean?" The Indian still held the tomahawk.

"It means when two people have similar interests, and they get along together. They like spending time with each other."

"You mean like Katie and my dad?"

My head jerked up and I squinted at the cowboy. "What makes you say that, young man?"

"You are only calling me young man, because you don't know which twin I am."

"Of course I know. You are Jack, I think. Now why did you say that?" In the corner of my eye I saw an Indian shinnying up a tree, head dress and all.

"Because Katie looks at my dad all gushy. You don't. That's because Katie and my dad are capible."

Flopping to the ground, I leaned against a tree. "So what should we do about it?" I was seeking the wisdom of a seven year old and only trying to envision what these kids would be like when they were ten.

"Tell him the truth, what else?"

What else indeed.

# Chapter 43

Some of the customers at work had been talking about a new movie that had come out, "Back to the Future". So when Reid called again, I suggested seeing a movie. Always the gentlemen, he arrived at the door bearing beautiful white and yellow daisies. Motioning him in, I told him I wasn't quite ready, but he could go in the kitchen and keep Katie company. Going as slow as I felt would be feasible, I said I quick prayer and headed for the kitchen. Katie was leaning against the counter; cheeks flushed a lovely rose color. Reid was talking animatedly, telling something funny which made Katie laugh. Looking closer, I understood what Jack was saying. There was a gushy look on her face, and I knew that I was doing the right thing.

The scheming twins and I did all we could to keep Reid and Katie in close contact at the theatre. The twins sitting on either side of me snickered when Katie and Reid were forced to sit next to each other. After a few minutes, Jack asked if I could take him and Jerry to the bathroom. After that, it was an urgent need for popcorn, then licorice, then the bathroom again. Although I was engrossed in the movie, I knew I was sacrificing for a good thing. After the second time to the bathroom, neither Reid nor Katie seemed to even notice that we were back.

Jack and Jerry must have lain awake at night conspiring plotting and planning, because the depth of their conspiring amazed even me. It couldn't have been even a month later when an uncomfortable Reid asked if I could meet him after work at the park. "I'd love to."

Reid was pacing anxiously as I pulled up in Monte, my old friend who was nearing its last leg (or tire). Reid was wearing a light blue chambray shirt with tan khaki's. He was a handsome man, and it was a bit disconcerting that his heart had been riveted so easily. But I had realized that my heart was not my own to give away. Someone still held a piece of it. Someday my heart would heal, but not yet. Katie was a worthy recipient of Reid's love, and I was happy for her.

Watching the confident business man stumbling over his words, wringing his hands and wearing an agonized expression, I thought it best to put him out of his misery.

"Reid, I think we both know that our relationship isn't going anywhere. Our opinions and lifestyles are very different. I'm more than aware of how your boys feel about me, and how they feel about Katie." With that statement his head bounced up and his eyes bored through my head. "You are a special man, Reid, and I truly hope that you will stay my friend and be a part of our family for a long time." Giving him a sisterly hug, I watched in amusement as his facial expression changed from trepidation to relief.

"How did you know?" His controlled manner was returning.

"It's just a gushy feeling I had." With a quick wave, I hopped back in my car. Watching Reid leave the park before me, I was left with mixed emotions. I too had a sense of relief, but also that haunting feeling of loneliness was creeping back in. Watching couples and families playing, picnicking, and belonging to someone left me feeling hollow, and empty inside. I had just watched my chance at happiness drive away, yet I knew there was only One who could satisfy and bring contentment, and I would have to trust in Him for my past, present and future.

# Chapter 44

Work kept me busy, as the warmth of the summer sun waned and the stately oak and maple foliage morphed into its autumn colors of brilliant reds and burnished orange. Being used to the summer rays waking me up in the morning, I was struggling to climb out of bed when it was still dark outside. Fumbling for the light switch, I was horrified to see how late it was getting. No time for makeup this morning, I whined. And no time to iron my uniform. Running my fingers through my long hair, I quickly braided it into what looked like a thick hemp rope.

Squealing in to the parking lot, I spotted Scotty, a patron and faithful customer since the restaurant first opened many years ago, greeted me with a meaningful glance at his watch. "I know, Scotty," I blurted as I sprinted to the front door. "I'm still trying to get used to these dark mornings. Is my boss here yet?"

"Nope, I think you beat him here. But another guy was asking for ya."

"Oh, don't tell me old cantankerous Henry Potts is up already."

"Nope, someone I never saw before. Nice looking young feller. Wanted to know what section was yours. Knew you by name."

A slow drum beat started beating in my head. Turning slowly around, I questioned him. "What does he look like?"

"Go see for yourself. He's been here since early this morning." Glued to where I stood, I forced the hammering in my head to slow down. But it only beat faster and stronger. Taking a deep breath, I swung open the door and surveyed the room with one quick swipe.

*Brad.* Sitting in my section in a corner booth. My heart burst into a colorful display of fireworks when I quickly tried to memorize every detail of his face in case the marvelous colors of light faded into another illusion of my mind. My legs turned to jelly as I willed them to keep moving. Walking as if in a dream, I pulled open a drawer, took out a clean apron, and carefully tied it around my waist. I took extra care to tie the strings in a neat bow. Grabbing a mug and coffee pot, I continued on in my nebulous journey toward the man who had never left my thoughts. The man who had captured my heart with his slow lazy smile. The only man I have ever known who could stir me so passionately with his pure maleness, and make me glad I was a woman. Brad, who could read into my soul and love me anyway. I plunked down the cup at his table and with two hands steadied the coffee pot as I poured the black liquid in his cup with quaking hands.

"Good morning, Brad. Are you in the mood for pancakes or eggs?"

# Epilogue

I'm sitting on the deck of my mountain home, watching the yellow moon climb over the mountaintop, with tall pine trees silhouetted against the dark. The stars are brilliant lights in the sky, and I can't help but think of the verse in Isaiah,

*Lift your eyes and look to the heavens: Who created all these? He who brings out the starry host one by one, and calls them each by name. Because of his great power and mighty strength, not one of them is missing.*

In the peacefulness of the moment, my mind wonders to the bedroom where two precious miracles lay sleeping, one boy and one girl. I pictured Faith curled up with her favorite blankie, a head full of silky blonde curls, and beautiful green eyes like her father's. Daniel makes me laugh with his zest for life, as if everything he does ends in an exclamation point. And then my mind drifts back to an Easter, years ago now, where a doctor told me that I may never have children. But he didn't know that God would work an incredible miracle of grace. I feel a warm tear roll down my cheek. The tear is not from sorrow, but of a joy so deep welling up within me. I hear Brad in the kitchen making popcorn. He will soon join me, and I will whisper my delicious secret to him. In seven months we will have child number three. Brad is such a good daddy. I know he will embrace another child in our home with love as he so easily has our first two.

Then an image of my own dad gently makes its way into my mind. So, I eventually realized that my dad is human after all. He has his faults, as we all do. He missed my mom too, and found a comfort in Victoria. I asked my father for forgiveness, and in that gesture, I have found a wonderful father, and the freedom that comes with forgiving. Victoria, who won't ever replace my mother, has become a friend, and I am thankful what a blessing she is to my father. They travel out west when they can and embrace the gift of grand parenting.

Eventually my mind roams to my heavenly Father. He taught me what real unconditional love is, which has allowed me to love freely in return. He put a new song in my mouth. Even praise to His name! And even more, He showed me mercy and grace. No songs have been written about me, or monuments dedicated to me. I'm just an average woman as the world would see me. But I have known what it is to be loved so deeply, to love another with my whole heart and that makes me special.

*Amazing grace, how sweet the sound*
*That saved a wretch like me*
*I once was lost, but now I'm found*
*Was blind but now I see.*

## Individual or Group Study Questions

1. *Circumstances have caused Grace to become bitter towards God and others. Has there been anything in your life that may have caused you to feel angry toward God? Have you resolved the issue? If yes, how would you encourage others who are struggling with blaming God or feeling anger? If issues have not been resolved, what is holding you back from enjoying sweet fellowship with God?*

2. *Has there been a time in your life when you thought taking care of things in your own way was the answer to solve a problem? Grace believed having an abortion would be the best way of taking care of her problem. How can seeking our own wisdom and understanding lead us down wrong paths?*

3. *Although Grace wanted to be able to freely love Brad, what was holding her back? Do your insecurities or feelings of inadequacy ever cause you to make choices that may not be the right ones?*

4. *In one day, Grace went from being very happy, to being angry and hurt. Have you ever over-reacted to situations where someone may have said something that hurt or disappointed you?*

5. *Brad wasn't sure that befriending Grace was the right thing to do. What do you think?*

6. *There are times in our lives when we think God is leading us to a decision or action. When Grace felt that Reid was more suited to her than Brad because he had a readymade family, she eventually realized she was wrong. How can we know God's will in our lives?*

Made in the USA
Lexington, KY
25 April 2012